Billion-Dollar Matches

The one thing money can't buy? Love!

Finding true love is *never* easy. But when you're famous, it's even harder... So, M is here to help! M is a dating agency with a twist. They offer, to the rich and famous, a chance to date away from the limelight. And it's this promise of absolute discretion that compels *every* A-lister to keep them on speed dial.

M's founder, Madison Morgan, is no stranger to the red carpet herself. A former child actress, Madison knows—better than anyone!—the value of privacy. Which makes her an expert at finding the *most* idyllic and secluded locations for her clients. From Lake Geneva to the Seychelles, and Puerto Rico to Indonesia, Madison creates the perfect backdrop to a couple's love story. And, just maybe, her own?

Fall in love with...

The Princess and the Rebel Billionaire
by Sophie Pembroke

Surprise Reunion with His Cinderella
by Rachael Stewart

Available now!

Caribbean Nights with the Tycoon
by Andrea Bolter

Indonesian Date with the Single Dad
by Jessica Gilmore

Coming soon!

Dear Reader,

It feels strange writing this to you in the thick of 2020 and the days of COVID-19, where nationwide or local lockdowns are never far away. Just leaving the house is a huge deal, leaving the country an impossible dream.

But this book was my escape, taking me to the gorgeous Seychelles and the fictitious island of Rosalie. Stunning aquamarine waters, magnificent granite boulders, beaches of powder-white sand, vibrant flora and fauna—all of it heaven-like. It was a joy to escape there with Jasmine and Freddie, and their second-chance romance was a delight to write.

I do hope it can provide you with the same reassuring warmth it gave me and bring many a happy smile to your face, and that the world, when this book finds you, is in a much better place.

You can always find yourself a happy-ever-after in between the pages of a Harlequin, and we've never needed these tales more.

"Stay safe and well" has been the motto for months now, so I'll say that and add a dollop of love, too!

Happy reading!

Rachael xx

Surprise Reunion with His Cinderella

Rachael Stewart

—

Special thanks and acknowledgment are given to
Rachael Stewart for her contribution to the
Billion-Dollar Matches miniseries.

HARLEQUIN®

Romance™

Recycling programs
for this product may
not exist in your area.

ISBN-13: 978-1-335-40671-2

Surprise Reunion with His Cinderella

For questions and comments about the quality of this book,
please contact us at CustomerService@Harlequin.com.

Harlequin Enterprises ULC
22 Adelaide St. West, 40th Floor
Toronto, Ontario M5H 4E3, Canada
www.Harlequin.com

Printed in U.S.A.

Rachael Stewart adores conjuring up stories, from heartwarmingly romantic to wildly erotic. She's been writing since she could put pen to paper—as the stacks of scrawled-on pages in her loft will attest to. A Welsh lass at heart, she now lives in Yorkshire, with her very own hero and three awesome kids—and if she's not tapping out a story, she's wrapped up in one or enjoying the great outdoors. Reach her on Facebook, Twitter (@rach_b52) or at rachaelstewartauthor.com.

Books by Rachael Stewart

Harlequin Romance

Tempted by the Tycoon's Proposal

Harlequin DARE

Mr. One-Night Stand
Mr. Temptation
Naughty or Nice
Getting Dirty
Losing Control
Unwrapping the Best Man
Our Little Secret
Reawakened

Visit the Author Profile page
at Harlequin.com for more titles.

For you, Aunty Carolyn.

For always believing in me and reading every
book I've ever written, even when they were in my
handwritten scrawl many moons ago!

Love always,

Rachael xx

Praise for
Rachael Stewart

"This is a delightful, moving, contemporary
romance.... I should warn you that this is the sort of
book that once you start you want to keep turning
the pages until you've read it. It is an enthralling
story to escape into and one that I thoroughly
enjoyed reading. I have no hesitation in highly
recommending it."

—*Goodreads* on *Tempted by the Tycoon's Proposal*

PROLOGUE

JASMINE WRUNG HER hands together. 'I'm not sure this is a good idea, Freddie.'

'It needs to be done.'

'But now?'

Nervously she bit into her lip and reached for his hand, tugging him away from the doors that led into the manor's great hall.

The noise from the other side ebbed and flowed with music and chatter, the clinking of glasses, the sound of laughter. The Highgrove Boxing Day party was in full swing. Friends, relatives and staff all gathering to enjoy the centuries-old tradition of handing out gifts and enjoying the festivities.

'It's your parents' big day.' She tried again. 'They love this party.'

'*I* love this party.'

Freddie turned to look down at her, his foppish dark hair curling over his forehead and softening the sharp cut of his tux. Didn't matter that she'd known him for ever, her breath still caught as she took his handsome face, his dreamy blue eyes all alive with his excitement.

She loved him. Loved him too much to refuse him, but *this*?

She toyed with her sleeves, their bell shape the

reason the dress had caught her eye in the charity shop window. Its medieval style fitted her petite frame perfectly, enhancing her subtle curves and gaining Freddie's wholehearted approval in the process. But now…now it just felt cheap and out of place.

'Everyone is here,' she whispered, her voice starting to fail her.

'Isn't that the point?' He combed his fingers through her hair, pressed his forehead to hers. 'Come on, Red. Isn't it time you got some fire to match your blazing hair?'

Was it? She chewed the corner of her mouth and tried to lose herself in his gaze, to let it work its magic. To warm her heart, ease her fear…

'I'm sick of them denying us, Red. I'm sick of the staff whispering about us. I'm sick of being made to feel like we're doing something wrong, like we should be ashamed. Doing it this way, they will have no choice but to acknowledge our relationship, to accept it. And we can look to the future, *our* future.'

A shiver trickled down her spine. Her mother was one of the staff. She too would witness what was about to happen. And she didn't want to make trouble for her. She'd been the Highgrove housekeeper for seventeen years. They'd employed her when others had passed her over for being a single mum with a one-year-old to provide for, so in a way Jasmine owed them too.

But Freddie was right, they'd tried to gain acceptance quietly and no one had taken them seriously. What choice did they have?

'I love you, Red.'

Her heart soared with his emphatic declaration, her love for him swamping all else as a smile broke through. 'I love you too, Freddie.'

'And it's time the world knew it, yes?'

She nodded and he lifted her left hand to his lips, kissed the tip of the diamond ring she should be used to wearing after six months. But tonight it felt heavy, weighed down by what they were about to do.

'I can't wait,' he whispered over the stone, his eyes catching hers as she took a courage-seeking breath.

She wished she could have his confidence, but then it was always this way. Freddie was the adventurous one, forever pushing her to come out of her shell. Though she wouldn't be able to hide behind him once they broke through those doors, hand in hand.

'Hey, you want to be Mrs Freddie Highgrove, right?'

He straightened, his eyes still hooked on hers, and she felt the colour bloom in her cheeks, the excited flutter in her heart—*Mrs Freddie Highgrove*.

'More than anything.'

He took both her hands in his and squeezed softly. 'Then trust me…'

CHAPTER ONE

JASMINE WALKER STARED out at the tropical paradise beyond the floating white drapes that framed her serene, picture-perfect view, and clutched both hands to her fluttering stomach.

It was just nerves.

Nerves she should be able to deal with.

It wasn't as though her livelihood was on the line.

It wasn't as though she was heading into a critical investors' meeting.

And it wasn't as though she was standing before the stern face of Highgrove senior, having just been caught stealing from Maggie's tray of freshly baked goods. Or worse, standing outside the doors to their great hall preparing for Freddie to announce their engagement.

So why couldn't she get a handle on this?

And why on earth was she even thinking of the Highgroves now, and a ten-year-old memory at that?

She swallowed, closed her eyes and forced her hands to relax. She breathed in the soft fragrance of her room. Subtle and deceptively simple, its floral notes were designed to instil a sense of calm, something she could certainly do with now as her body tripped over itself.

You know why you're thinking of them—thinking of him—so quit kidding yourself...

She opened her eyes, and saw the answer in everything around her, everything she heard. The suite with its mix of wood, soft cream furnishings and colourful creole art. The private terrace with its king-sized thatched cabana and the infinity pool that dropped off into the endless turquoise sea beyond. The lulling sound of the waves and the native wildlife.

It was a secluded oasis designed for romance and relaxation. For lovers. For honeymooners...

Of all the places the M dating agency to the rich and famous could have sent her on this crazy, outrageous week-long blind date, they had chosen here.

The Seychelles.

The one place Freddie Highgrove, her childhood friend, her teenage heartthrob, her one and only love, had promised to take her. And not just for a holiday, but for their honeymoon.

A bittersweet smile touched her lips and she dropped onto the plush mattress behind her, lay back and stared up at the netted roof to her four-poster bed.

*Freddie. S*he breathed in his name and let it out with all the guilt, the remorse, the sadness. It was a lifetime ago, but she felt it all like yesterday. He was the reason every one of her relationships failed.

No one could stack up to the wild intensity of the naïve passion they'd shared.

The day their relationship had crossed over from friends to lovers had marked the start of a whirlwind affair that had seen Freddie proposing on her eighteenth birthday. The memory was so perfect and yet not, because it had heralded the beginning of the end.

She hadn't been good enough, and that version of her—the insecure, shy little wallflower—had run. She had loved Freddie too much to bear the rejection of his family or, worse, to see him rejecting them.

It was time to let that version of her go.

Only…she wasn't so sure that being matched by M was the answer.

Decisions made on nights out with your rowdy and far more adventurous girlfriends had a tendency to go a little pear-shaped. And of all those decisions, this was the most expensive and riskiest to date.

It was insane. One hundred thousand pounds and then some, insane.

As though her friends, Sadie and Izzy, could sense her rising doubts, her phone buzzed beside her. Sadie, the main instigator of this whole trip, had dropped a message into their group chat.

You there yet? Have you met him? What's he like? Please tell me he's hot. Like seriously hot!

She smiled, in spite of the continued butterflies and tapped in her reply.

Yes. No. Now, shh!

Sadie's response was instant, her fingers like lightning thanks to all the practice.

Then text in a timely fashion and I won't need to nag!

Jasmine shook her head.

Yes, Mum.

Then:

Have fun. xxxxx And don't do anything I wouldn't do!

'Yeah, right!' Jasmine laughed. 'From you, that means do everything and anything, Sades!'

She tossed her phone aside and shook her head all the more. *This* was the kind of crazy thing Sadie would do. Not her.

'Not sensible, boring, workaholic, need-to-get-a-life Jasmine.'

She shuddered as she remembered those exact words spilling from Sadie's lips and Izzy's vigorous nod of agreement. But her friends were right. She did need to get a life outside work.

But now she was here…and so was he. Her 'perfect match' according to M. And of the hundreds and thousands of possible destinations, they were in the Seychelles.

She'd asked for somewhere hot. She'd asked for somewhere without too much digital interference—she should have specified no mobile phone signal on top of it and then she wouldn't have to cope with friend inference either.

Truth was, she'd wanted a holiday, a break from it all, but *the Seychelles*…

She swallowed again, pushing the resurfacing Freddie from her mind and her heart.

It was no good being stuck in the past. This was about the future, *her* future. And if M said they had her match, then she owed it to them and to her bank balance to make the most of it.

Plus, Sadie and Izzy would never let her live it down if she bailed.

Her mobile buzzed with a new message and she sat up, taking it with her. It was Izzy.

Hope you had a good journey! Now enjoy and keep us posted! xx PS Sades, back off! ;-*

Jasmine grinned and started to type a response but a rap at the door sent her stomach somersaulting and her fingers stilled over her phone screen.

Another rap. 'Miss Walker, it's Monique, I'm here to take you to dinner.'

Oh, God. She shot up off the bed, wiped her hot and clammy hands on the little black dress she'd chosen and sucked in another breath. If she kept taking breaths like this she'd faint from an overdose of oxygen.

'Miss Walker, are you there? Your perfect match awaits!'

Perfect match. Another gulp and she clutched a hand to the locket that she wore, the locket that contained a photo of her late mother. *She who dares, wins,* came her mother's voice.

'Coming,' she blurted.

Taking one last scan of her serene room, her safe haven for the week, she told herself how perfect it was. That no matter who her date was, this week was a holiday and she hadn't had one of those in a long time.

She walked to the door, pulling it open to see the petite woman who had shown her to her room earlier. She was lovely. Deep brown skin, warm conker-brown eyes and a big smile.

'Thank you for coming to get me.'

'It's my pleasure. If you'd like to follow me… Tonight you are dining at the lighthouse.'

She offered her a smile over her shoulder, and Jasmine tried to return it, trapping the squeak-like hum that threatened to erupt.

She tried to focus instead on what she was seeing, the raw wooden floor, the soothing cream walls, the colourful artwork and the various plants, all much the same as her suite. Monique herself was the picture of sunshine, her button-down dress a lemon-yellow, her hair pulled back from her face by a floral band, and her white slip-on shoes flat and quiet as she walked. Jasmine's gold heels, on the other hand, click-clacked with a deafening resonance, her dress feeling too clingy and cloying.

Or was it more that her senses were in tingling overdrive as she fretted over the person she was about to meet?

It had taken M months to find him—*months!* She'd almost forgotten she'd signed up for the service when the email had pinged to say they had her match... Okay, so she'd *tried* to forget but, still, here she was...with him.

Just him.

On an entire island that was theirs for the duration. Rosalie Island. It even sounded romantic. The only other people here were the Golden Key resort staff, on hand to cater to their every whim...

At least her match had been properly vetted. A properly vetted man couldn't turn out to be some axe-wielding serial killer. A possibility she'd thrown at Sadie and Izzy who'd both just rolled their eyes and blamed the crazy notion on her overactive imagination. They had then reminded her of the ridiculous sum each client had to pay up front and suggested that at least he would be a very *rich* axe murder who didn't need to feast off her wealth.

But who exactly *was* her perfect match? She certainly didn't know, and there was a part of her curious to find out.

Only one man had ever come close to perfect…

'Freddie. Freddie. Freddie.'

Both Sadie and Izzy were in her head again, rolling their eyes dramatically.

'Forget about Freddie!'

And they were right. She could not—*would* not—compare her match to him like she had every other partner she'd been involved with over the years. She had to stop.

The love one felt as a teenager, that first love—the lust, the heat, the newness of it all—made it intense. It had the power to sweep you off your feet. But she was an adult now, she didn't need a fairy tale.

And waiting for her at the lighthouse was a man who could potentially be 'the one'.

But therein lay the rub.

She had zero expectation that they'd found him.

In fact, Jasmine Walker was convinced 'the one' just wasn't out there…

Or he was…but she ruined her chance with that particular man a long, long time ago.

What are you doing?

Freddie Highgrove let his gaze drift from the

pretty white brick lighthouse to the impressive vista beyond. With the sun hanging low in the sky it cast everything it touched in a warm amber glow. The endless sea, the luscious vegetation, the white sand beach with its rolling granite boulders breaking into the water. It was all so very easy on the eye and he tried to feel nothing. Nothing at all.

But the grip he had over his chilled glass mimicked the tight hold around his heart and both told him otherwise.

There was only one woman he'd ever intended to travel here with.

Jasmine Walker. The one that had got away. The one that had *run* away, even.

The moment the pilot of the private jet arranged by the M dating agency had announced their destination, he should have ordered them to stay grounded and let him make his exit. Quick, sharp, painless.

Instead, he was waiting on the arrival of said date with a bitter taste in his mouth and no amount of the island's chilled finest could see it off.

It was his own sorry fault too. Not M's.

When Madison Morgan, the owner and very much the heart of M, had asked *'When I say romance, what location do you think of first?'* he should have ducked it. Not said the first thing that had come into his dim-witted brain.

He gave a brutal laugh, the sound as harsh as it had been when she'd posed the question.

The Seychelles.

He could have said Paris, Rome—anywhere else—but no.

And why? Because of her. Jasmine.

Ten years and he couldn't rid himself of the woman. And she hadn't even been a woman then, not really. They'd been teenagers counting on a future so rosy it made him feel sick to think of it now. Sick and foolish.

He rubbed his freshly shaven jaw and tilted his head back to the setting sun. Now there wasn't a romantic bone left in his body, he had no interest. No interest in a date of M's choosing, or a marriage of convenience designed to elevate his illustrious family's reputation.

So, what on earth was he doing here?

His lips quirked. He knew what he was doing, all right. He was delaying the inevitable, putting off his Scottish parents' wish that he marry into the English aristocracy by convincing them he was finding his own 'rich' and 'suitably entitled' wife.

He ran a finger through the collar of his black polo shirt, the fabric, though breathable, felt too thick and heavy as he wished he was anywhere but here. Anywhere but about to sit down with some unsuspecting woman who through no fault of her own could never be the one for him. Regardless of what M may think.

Truth was, what heart he'd possessed had left

with Jasmine ten years ago. And try as they might, his parents were going to be sorely disappointed if they were depending on his marriage to enhance their place in the world. As for grandkids, more lairds-in-waiting, it wasn't happening.

Ten years ago—*yes*. It was all he'd wanted. Marriage. Kids. A family home filled with love and warmth. He would have taken that over his family's wealth and status any day. But Jasmine had bailed on him.

Fifteen years of friendship. A year as lovers. A ring on her finger. And it hadn't been enough to make her stay and fight.

His hand pulsed around his glass and he threw back the chilled liquid, not tasting a drop. He wouldn't be that fool again.

'Mr Highgrove?'

He turned at Monique's voice, forcing a smile, and—

No.

He had to be seeing things.

It wasn't.

It couldn't be.

'May I present Miss—'

'Jas!' It choked out of him. This had to be some kind of sick and twisted joke.

The Jasmine lookalike gasped, her hand flying to her mouth, her eyes—those eyes that had haunted his dreams, his nightmares too—wide.

'Freddie?'

Monique frowned. 'You two…' she looked at Jasmine, looked at him '…know each other?'

He couldn't respond. He felt like every grain of sand on the beach had made its way into his lungs, his chest, his body. He couldn't breathe.

Monique cleared her throat. 'It seems I needn't introduce you after all.' She clasped her hands together, her eyes dancing in the golden light. 'How clever M has been on this occasion! Do please take a seat, Miss Walker.' She gestured to Jasmine's chair like the tension weighing heavy in the air didn't exist. How could she not feel it? He couldn't even move for it and neither could Jasmine. Her mouth was still agape, her pallor obvious in spite of her make-up and the warm glow of the evening.

'I shall pour the champagne,' Monique said as Jasmine stayed stock-still.

'No.'

Both women jumped and Monique's eyes narrowed on him. The 'no' had come from him… *Oh, this wasn't good.*

'Excuse me, sir?'

'What I mean is…' He softened his voice, working hard to relax his posture, but his heart was pounding, his pulse beating wild at the sight of Jasmine. His first glimpse in ten years, and it wasn't just a glimpse, *she* was his date! 'I will pour it.'

'Of course.' If Monique still considered his

behaviour odd, she made no show of it as she beamed. 'I will leave you to get reacquainted and bring your starters out when they are ready.'

She walked away, her whispered words carrying on the breeze. 'Well, well, well, this has to be a first.'

A first he could have done without...

'Take a seat, Jas.' He waved his empty hand at her chair before pulling out his own. 'I won't bite.'

He couldn't look at her as he said it, though. He was in shock. Utter shock.

'Did you set this up?' she whispered.

A laugh erupted through his chest, his eyes soaring to hers. 'Are you serious?'

She was. He could see it in the accusatory glint to her brilliant green eyes, her glossy pink lips pursed.

This couldn't be real.

Only it was...

'Do you honestly think that of all the women in the world I would choose to bring you here?'

As intended, his words stung. He watched with forced satisfaction as her eyes flared and her throat bobbed. That beautiful slender throat in that petite little frame that had hardly grown in the time they'd been apart.

Compared to his six feet one, was she still only five feet three?

He remembered the day he'd measured her, pressed up against the wall of the kitchen in Highgrove Manor. Her refusing to believe that he was almost a foot taller than her, him proving a point, while enjoying every inch of her body trapped against his.

He breathed past the sudden rush of tension, the lustful hit the silly little memory sparked, and dragged his eyes from the alluring green of hers.

'No, Jas.' Like it needed stating in clearer terms. 'I did not set this up.'

He reached for the champagne and poured two glasses, the gentle fizz of the drink as it bubbled up in the glass more pronounced for the silence now stretching between them.

And still she hadn't moved.

He rested the bottle back in the ice and looked at her. Her blazing red hair was cut into a long, smooth bob that smacked of both sophistication and maturity. The black dress she wore clung to her curves and ended just above her knee with the smallest of front slits, and a pair of gold heels that gave her an added inch or two.

Classic. Smart. Disturbingly stunning.

And aside from her obvious shock, there was a confidence about her, an unfamiliar poise that made him shift in his seat.

'I take it from the persistent shock on your face that you didn't set this up either?'

'How could I possibly...?' She shook her head, her arms folding around her middle in a protective gesture that dug beneath his skin, wounding as much as it angered. It wasn't him that had broken her heart. It wasn't her that needed the protection.

And neither do you...you're older and wiser and know better.

'No.' She wet her lips. 'I didn't set this up.'

'In that case, why don't you sit, and we'll offer up a toast to this cruel twist of fate.'

She eyed him, wary and silent. Long, drawn-out moments when he thought she might turn and run—*again*.

But finally she stepped towards him, her scent carrying on a sudden breeze, and his chest spasmed.

How can she still smell the same?

He raised a hand to his face, a barrier to her scent as he masked it with his own and watched her lower herself into the chair opposite. He didn't want to feast on the sight of her up close, of the flames from the firepit in the centre of the viewing platform flickering in her eyes, dancing over her skin and making her hair even more vibrant.

He sought distraction in the drinks he'd poured and took up hers, offering it to her. He realised his mistake the second her delicate fingers brushed against his. Their eyes collided and for the briefest of moments time fell away. They were in the Highgrove guest house, the fire roaring, a diamond ring fresh on her finger, champagne in hand.

He gritted his teeth and retreated back into his chair, taking his drink with him.

'To us.' He raised his glass to her, the vulnerability in her eyes holding him captive, and inwardly winced. He could practically feel her reaching inside his soul and stamping all over it anew.

'To…' She swallowed and wet her cupid's-bow lips. 'To us.'

CHAPTER TWO

THE CHAMPAGNE STUCK in Jasmine's throat as she lost herself in the sight of him.

Freddie. *Her* Freddie. The man whose heart she had broken, shattering her own in the process.

She'd been convinced he was a figment of her imagination. With the sun setting at his back, she'd tried to convince herself it wasn't him. That it couldn't be.

But it had been a sixth sense, a growing awareness that the man standing there, waiting for her, his smile as frozen as his body, was him.

She cleared her throat, swallowed with a gulp that she prayed wasn't audible and lost herself in the dark glittering gaze that was so familiar and yet not. Those blue eyes that had once sparkled with such humour, such love, such passion... now they were almost black, the flames from the firepit playing in their brooding depths.

She shuddered as the flutter in her stomach returned tenfold and she covered it with her palm.

'Cold, Jas?'

She shook her head, words refusing to form.

'I don't think I've ever known you to be lost for words, not in my presence at any rate.' His eyes narrowed on her. 'There was a time when you had plenty to say.'

His soft-spoken observation was all the more powerful for the past it recalled and the frostiness in the air that no amount of paradise could warm.

'It's just…it's a shock. It's been…' She broke off. She had the awful feeling her champagne was about to make a reappearance.

'Ten years,' he supplied for her. 'Ten years in December.'

She lowered her lashes, raised her glass to her lips and took a larger sip. If a small amount was threatening to return, maybe a larger amount would weigh itself down. And she needed the Dutch courage.

She felt eighteen again. Insecure. Out of place. Unworthy.

But she was none of those things any more. And, boy, did she need the timely reminder.

'How have you been, Freddie?' She forced her eyes back to his as she acknowledged just how much he'd changed too.

He wasn't the tall, athletic man of his youth. He was broad, sculpted, his voice deeper. His black hair, no longer foppishly long, was trimmed, tailored to fit his new persona—sharp, empowered, all man—and she shivered anew. He demanded attention, dominated her vision, made her feel things she'd long given up hope of feeling again.

He leaned back in his seat and rested his elbow on the arm of his chair as he ran his index finger over his lips. She tried not to watch, tried not to take in the fullness of that bottom lip, or feel the tingling sensation it sent through her body.

'I'm good. Very good.' His mouth lifted to the side, not quite a smile, his stare intense as he watched her. 'No need to ask how you are, I can see that well enough for myself.'

'Still…' Her hand trembled over her stomach and she lifted it to her hair, sweeping it back behind her ear as she raised her chin to him. 'It would be polite to ask.'

'Polite?' He surprised her with another laugh and leaned forward in his seat. Planting his elbows on the table, he steepled his fingers and rested his chin on them, his eyes pinning her in place.

'So, Jasmine…' He was too close now, much too close. His aftershave—expensive, masculine, woody—reached her and her nostrils flared, panic lifting the hairs at her nape. 'How the devil are you?'

The question reverberated down her spine as her heart tried to clamber up and out of her throat. She didn't like how he said it, his Scottish high-born inflection colliding with an American twang and making him so far removed from the boy she once knew.

But then he wasn't the boy trying to be a man any more, the boy so willing to reject his family for her, offering to run away and make a new life with her.

No.

He had his own wealth now, his own life across the Pond, and everything about him spoke of that new existence, of that independence and liberation. But his eyes... His eyes still showed the broken heart she'd left him with and it was that which held her tongue-tied.

Did he still hate her after all this time?

She hated herself enough for walking away. But she couldn't bear facing his hatred too.

'I think this is a mistake.' She started to rise. 'I'm sorry you've paid good money for this... *this...*'

Her hand flapped about, words failing her.

'Date?' He looked up at her, his eyes glinting, his mouth twitching. Was he laughing at her?

'Yes.' She tried to detach herself from the cocktail of emotion fogging up her brain. 'I'll contact M and see if something can be done.'

'Why?'

'Because you can't want to spend this week with me.'

'Why?'

She blew out a flustered breath, felt her cheeks heat with a combination of shame, panic, hurt, even anger that he would make her put words to it. 'You know why.'

She stepped away from the table.

'Running away again, Jas?'

She stilled. It was a low blow. But there was

something in his voice that made her pulse trip over itself, and not entirely with anger.

She wanted to stay. She wanted to show him that she wasn't the same person that left him ten years ago. She wanted to show him the person she had become. Confident. Successful. Worthy.

It no longer mattered what the Highgroves thought of her. Freddie included.

Yeah, like you really mean that...

'No.' She ignored the inner scorn. 'If you really must know, Freddie, I'm trying to salvage what we can of this week. Maybe M has another date in reserve for you, someone she can send out to accompany you so the week's not a total waste of your time and money, and I'll leave.'

Someone more accustomed to champagne and fine dining and the demands of a family as high-born as his own. Because it didn't matter that she had become a woman of standing. In their eyes she would never be worthy. She would always be the help's daughter.

'And what if I said I don't want someone else?'

Her eyes lifted to his. Her heart stuttered in her chest. He couldn't mean it.

But try as she might, she couldn't read his expression.

He looked serious, but his posture was far too relaxed to be genuine as he leaned back in his chair.

Or at least that was how she'd like to interpret it.

'Don't look so shocked.'

She shook her head, her laugh high-pitched as she eyed the view instead. The sun was almost gone, a sliver of bright amber radiating out across the waves, the sky, its soft hue so golden and warm. But she was cold. Chilled to the bone. 'You can't want to spend this week with me,' she repeated.

'On that you're very much mistaken.'

She met his gaze, confusion and apprehension making her frown. She couldn't deny the bubble of excitement, too, that against her better judgement she was getting carried away with the meaning behind his words.

'To be completely honest, Jas, now that you're here, I can't imagine anyone else I'd rather spend this week with.'

And, again, what on earth are you doing?

Maybe this question would hound him all week, because common sense, or rather his heart, told him to re-insert an ocean between them as soon as possible.

But then he hadn't been thinking clearly when he'd blurted it out. His only goal had been to avoid the alternative: her leaving and someone coming in her place.

Or, worse, her staying and him being replaced.

It was madness.

Ten years they'd gone without seeing one another. She could have married, had a thousand boyfriends, lovers, whatever and he shouldn't care. But now that she was here, in front of him, the idea of her being with anyone else...

And it was just a week. One week.

Seven days with the woman his parents had so cruelly rejected was an interesting twist of fate.

Seven days with the woman who had so cruelly rejected him in turn was even more twisted.

But where he had once been weak, he was now strong and here before him was the opportunity to lay the ghosts of the past to rest and finally get her out of his system. Move on. It was a sound plan. And he always liked to have a plan.

'What do you say, Jas?'

'What do I say to what?'

The line between her brows deepened and she caught the corner of her lip in her teeth just like she used to when she was on edge. It made his chest ache even as he shut the emotion down for what it was—ridiculously sentimental.

'One week together. We can catch up, and then we can go our separate ways again.'

'You can't be serious?'

He raised his hand palm up and shrugged. 'I don't see why not.'

She continued to flounder, quiet and contemplative, and he forced himself to act as though he wasn't perturbed in the slightest. Not even a bit.

'After all, we always wanted to visit the Sey-chelles.'

Her eyes glistened, and his skin prickled, his chest quick to tighten. Was she going to cry?

He started to straighten, blinked once, and weak Jasmine was gone, replaced by a pale, stone-faced replica. He settled back once more. Better. This was better. *This* version he could cope with.

'That was a long time ago, Freddie.'

'Indeed. We've both grown up a lot since then…' He let his eyes travel over her, memo-ries heating up his body, tightening up his core. Her chest lifted under his appraisal, the pulse in her throat fluttering as her cheeks coloured. They still had it. The spark. It arced between them just as readily as it had back then. 'It could even be quite…enjoyable.'

'Enjoyable?' She choked over it. Her eyes wild. Her laugh sudden. 'Are you crazy?'

'No, I'm not crazy, Jas.' He stared back at her, determined, hungry. 'I'm a man used to taking the opportunities life throws my way.'

'And you see me—*this*—as an opportunity?'

'Definitely.' His lips quirked. He wanted to laugh at her outright horror. Provoking her was something he could definitely enjoy. The potent mix of anger and lust had him feeling more alive than he had in years.

And now that he was over his shock, he couldn't think of a better way to spend the next seven days. A little reacquaintance, testing the chemistry that so obviously still fizzed and pulsed between them…

'Seven days getting to know one another again, each other's likes, dislikes…'

He let the suggestion hang in the air, ran his index finger beneath his lip and watched her eyes flit to the move, the heat so obvious in their depths. She was shaking her head, but the rest of her…

'You can't seriously hope to just pick up where we left off?' She lifted a hand to the gold locket she wore, clutched it to her chest. 'We were practically kids, Freddie, kids with naïve expectations of how life could be.'

'True. And now we're adults. Our eyes wide open to the wonders of the world and its harsh reality. In all honesty, I have no time or need for a relationship. Pleasure, on the other hand…'

Her sucked-in breath made him want to laugh all the more, laugh and kill off the rising heat deep within his gut. He was playing with fire and if he wasn't careful, he'd be the one burned. That was if she didn't take flight first…

'We hired M to find us a love match, Freddie, a *relationship*! *You paid* for that. Not for a week of…of…' She gesticulated, looking so deliciously flustered he had the urge to grab one flapping hand and tug her onto his lap, to seal her parted lips with his.

Would she still taste the same?

'Sex, Jas. You can say it.'

She clamped her mouth shut, clutched the locket tighter. He wondered whether it housed a photo. And if so, whose...?

'May I remind you...' he lifted his eyes back to hers, halting his thoughts, which were getting too personal '...you also paid for a love match.'

Her nose flared with her breath. 'Only because my friends wouldn't leave me well alone.'

Now he laughed, until it hit him that her confession relieved him far too much. 'In that case, it's definitely a win-win.'

She pressed her lips together and her eyes started to dance. Her shock and panic were dissipating, replaced with something that looked far more like amusement. 'You really are serious?'

'Always.'

Her lips started to curve up, her head shake became softer, one of wonder and possibility.

'And let's be honest, Jas, the way I see it, M hasn't really failed. Seems Madison Morgan is actually rather skilled.'

'But don't you want to see who else she has out there for you? Don't you—?'

'What I want...' He grimaced as her eyes widened and he realised his exasperation at life, his parents and their expectations had erupted with his interjection. He tried again. 'What I want is a week away from my interfering family. A week

to forget the world exists outside these islands. A week to forget our past and just have fun, enjoy ourselves.'

He watched her frown ease, her hand lowering to her side as her eyes softened with what looked too much like compassion and he had to look away. He didn't want to *feel* around her, not in that way. He'd handed her the reins to his heart long ago, and he wouldn't do that again.

'Let's be clear,' he stated, wanting to avoid any potential misunderstanding. 'I had no intention of coming here for love, Jas. I was foolish enough to fall in love once and that was enough. This week was about putting my parents and their matchmaking schemes on the back burner for a while. Buying myself some time, so to speak.'

Her throat bobbed, realisation dawning and dousing the flush to her skin. 'Still so desperate to marry you off to a lady of status and means, are they?'

There was a tease to her voice, her words, but he wasn't blind to the fact she was trying to cover up a pain of old.

'Won't they always?'

Her lips parted, her shoulders lifting as she went to say something and stopped, her body deflating with her breath .

'What?' She was quiet. Too quiet, and he wanted to know. 'Jas?'

Maybe, for all she claimed to have been coaxed

into signing up to M, deep down she did want to find herself a man. And since he'd so clearly stated that man wasn't him, he'd ultimately ruined her week.

He hated that it had the power to hurt him. That ten years on she could get to him as easily as she had then. And yet he didn't even know her now.

Not quite true…

He knew plenty from the internet. How she'd become a rising star in the world of tech. How her app had made her millions. How it had made her clients successful too. She was an industry icon with the kind of money that made M's price tag a drop in the ocean.

But money and power told him nothing of the woman beneath the accolades…and he wanted that knowledge. He wanted to get to know the woman she was now. And that need should have had him running, but instead he was pushing for more.

So much for keeping away from the personal…

'Unless, of course, you'd prefer I leave so that M can send you their next candidate?'

'No.' She came alive, dropping back into her seat and burying her head in her hands.

She shook her head, her glossy red bob hypnotic in the light of the fire.

'But this is crazy, surreal even. I mean…' She raised her head, her eyes spearing him. 'It's you, Freddie! You!'

'It is.' His smooth voice belied the chaos within, the swarm of emotions that he couldn't get a handle on.

'I still can't believe this is really happening.'

He took a sip from his glass, waited until he knew his voice was steady. 'You'd better believe it, Red.'

Red.

His nickname for her. He shouldn't have used it. Shouldn't have, but he'd done it anyway, the name flowing off his tongue as easily as breathing and causing the colour to creep into her cheeks, spreading beneath the freckles that he remembered so well. Freckles that covered her creamy skin, top to toe. Would there be more now?

'Don't,' she breathed.

'Don't want?'

'Don't look at me like that.' She reached for her drink, took a gulp.

'Look at you like what?' He feigned innocence but he could feel the hunger so blatant through his body that it was sure to be blazing in his eyes too.

'Like...' Another swallow. 'Like you possess that X-ray vision you so often spoke of.'

He chuckled, the sound so throaty and thick he hardly recognised it as his own.

'If I remember rightly, you often wore the same expression...'

Her eyes raked over his chest, their green

depths dark and luscious and oh, so vivid as she appraised him.

'You're doing it now,' he murmured.

Her eyes collided with his. 'I blame you.'

'You hungry?'

Her lips parted, her cheeks flushing all the more. 'Freddie, I don't think this is a good idea.'

'Best not tell the chef…' His eyes flitted to the right, to where a smiling Monique was approaching. 'It would be a shame to tell Monique to turn around.'

'To tell…' She turned to follow his line of sight and instantly snapped back to him. 'You could have said!'

'I was having too much fun.'

CHAPTER THREE

SHE WAS TREADING a dangerous path. That much was obvious.

But could she walk away from him now?

No.

She knew the risks of what she was agreeing to. A week with him, like this. And with that look in his eye, she *knew* that he would want more from her than she could safely give.

Because he would never want her love, and she wasn't convinced she could give in to the lust heating the very air they breathed without falling deep.

But, then, who was to say she would love the man he was now? The man who still blamed her, hated her even, for what she'd done. The man who'd just declared he had no interest in love and labelled his younger self as foolish for having done so. This man's blue eyes didn't sparkle with easy teasing, or warm with love, or dance with happiness. There was an edge to his humour, a reservation to his remarks.

No, this man looked and behaved much more like his father. Cold and severe.

This man would hurt her as readily as he would take his first bite of the delicious meal being placed before them. She didn't doubt it for a second, so why was she still sitting here like some willing lamb off to the slaughter?

It was an impossible situation and as she eyed the exquisitely arranged dish and smiled up at Monique blankly, pretending to listen to what the woman was saying about the food, all she could really hear was the inner rant telling her to end it before it ended her. Extreme, but...

'Thank you, Monique,' Freddie said when Jasmine couldn't manage a word. 'This looks delicious.'

His eyes flicked to her and she smiled wider. 'Yes.' *Breathe!* 'Thank you.'

'Bon appétit.' Monique bowed her head and turned away, her muted footsteps loud in the sudden silence.

He picked up his cutlery and tucked in. All the while she watched him, his hum of appreciation filling her ears as she appreciated him. The masculine cut to his jaw as he moved the food around, his clean-shaven skin enhancing the dimple in his right cheek, the bob to his throat as he swallowed...

'You should try it,' he encouraged, so calm, so in control. 'It's delicious.'

She didn't think she'd be able to swallow anything past the swell of desire persisting irrespective of her fears, determined to torment her. And then it hit her: the spark she always attributed to being young and naïve, the power and intensity of one's first love—it wasn't down to that at all. It was him. Freddie.

He was the one who inspired those feelings in her, those feelings that no one else had come close to triggering. Not even Tim, her closest thing to an ex, and she'd almost married him.

'I meant what I said, Jasmine. I want us to make the most of this week. We're both cut off from the world and there's something to be said for having that kind of privacy, don't you agree?'

She considered his words, considered the way she felt inside. Reawakened. Hot. Wanton. As for her heart… She swallowed. Ten years she'd been haunted by their break-up. She'd not only lost her best friend, she'd lost the love of her life. Now they had a chance to make new memories, happier ones. A seven-day reset on ten years of pain.

She took up her glass, felt his eyes trace the movement as she sipped at her drink, forcing down the wedge in her throat, the panic and the thrill.

'Yes.' It was soft, barely audible. 'I agree.'

'So, let's make a pact.' He lifted his glass out to her, drawing her eyes to his, their magnetic sparkle sucking her in. Did it matter that it wasn't the same kind of sparkle? That there was an edge she couldn't dismiss? No. In fact, it helped keep this within the realms of reality, it would stop her getting carried away. 'We lay the ghosts of the past to rest and at the end of this week we go our separate ways. We move on.'

He made it sound so simple, but…

'Okay.' It caught in her throat, her tummy twisting in warning, but she smiled over it, gave a very definite nod.

His grin was worth every second of discomfort. The haunted look of Freddie that fateful Boxing Day ten years ago, when she'd walked away from him on the doorstep, was replaced for a split second by Freddie now. Pleased. Satisfied. Wanting her.

'You're on.' Smooth. Confident. Better. 'One week to forget it all. One week to just be.'

'Agreed.' His jaw pulsed, his eyes flashed, and he raised his glass to her. 'One week to just be.'

She clinked her glass to his and lost herself further in the intensity of his gaze. She took a sip of the champagne that sealed the deal and his eyes trailed lower. Following the journey of the chilled liquid as it glided down her throat, settling somewhere amongst the dizzying dance kicking off down low.

This was insane but she wasn't about to stop it.

For the first time in too long she was living for the now. Not for her business, not for her mum or her friends. Not even him.

Just her.

He couldn't take his eyes off her.

He was constantly noting what had changed, what was the same. Her accent had mellowed, much like his own, the curse of conversing with anyone outside Scotland, or even Edinburgh for that matter.

Her oval face was sharper, her cheekbones more pronounced. He watched as she played with her food and wondered whether she ate properly at all. Did she look after herself? What had changed over the years to bring about such change?

And the truth was, he didn't just wonder, he worried.

But he shouldn't be worrying. He was here for a week with a beautiful woman, and she was that, no more…if he were to adhere to their pact and forget the past.

M truly had outdone themselves. He'd given them a list as long as his arm, a challenge he'd never expected them to meet. And he certainly hadn't expected them to throw his past back in his face.

He was intrigued. What was it about Jasmine now that made her his 'perfect match' according to M?

'Do you not like it?' He gestured to her plate, to the barely touched prawn tartare and its equally delicious kiwi guacamole.

Her eyes flittered to his, her cheeks flushing and making her eyes appear greener, brighter.

'It's lovely.'

She covered her lips with her fingers, their dusty pink tips perfectly manicured, not bitten as they had been all those years ago. This Jasmine was more refined and yet still possessed the blushes and the edgy mannerisms of her youth.

'I'm just…' She frowned even as her lips curved up. 'This whole thing…it's crazy, unbelievable…'

'You're saying the shock of it has stolen your appetite?'

'I'm saying I'm distracted by it.' She picked up her glass of wine, a chilled Sémillon chosen to complement the dish, and smiled softly. 'You have to admit, it's a little surreal.'

'You've said that already.'

Her smile grew as she swallowed a considerable gulp. 'And I'm still coming to terms with it.'

'Well, let's pick it apart.'

She frowned. 'Pick it apart?'

'Yes, work out what we said to M to make us so perfect for one another.'

He didn't like saying 'perfect' out loud, it gave the idea merit, the idea of a relationship again merit…

Never going to happen.

'Okay,' she drawled.

'You start.'

'Me?' She arched those perfectly shaped brows at him—again, another change. He wondered how often she had her appearance tended to these days. She never used to be quite so careful with such things. 'Why me?'

'It's polite to let the woman go first.'

She laughed, the sound rippling through him with its familiarity, its authenticity. She was relaxing into this meal and he was glad of it, even as he felt his own defences lower.

'I can't even remember half the stuff I said to Madison now.'

'No?' It was his turn to arch his brows. 'I don't believe you.'

She pursed her lips, the fire flickering gold in her green eyes and making him want to lean in closer. 'You just want me to feed your ego.'

'Ah…' He cleared his throat as the sound caught, stuck by the lust he couldn't dampen. 'Guilty as charged. I indeed have an ego that likes the occasional stroking.'

'Like it ever really needed it.'

History passed between them again, a charged stillness where the air crackled and the years evaporated. They were young and easy again, teasing one another, having fun.

Until they weren't.

'Okay.' Discreetly, he shook off the chill. 'I'll start. We're both from Edinburgh.'

She laughed again, the sound just as tantalising, just as addictive, and he wanted to coax out more—more smiles, more lightness.

'We're the same age,' she fired back.

'You're older.'

'Hardly.' She shifted in her seat, sat straighter. 'There's two months between us!'

And there was that laugh again. It made his body warm from the inside out, an experience he rarely, if ever, felt these days. Her laugh tapered off as her lashes lowered to where his fingers toyed with the base of his wine glass. 'I wanted someone skilled with their hands.'

The husky edge to her voice set his blood on fire and he gave a soft chuckle. 'How forward.'

Her eyes snapped to his. 'Not like that.'

His lips twitched. 'No?'

'No! I meant…you know, creative, arty. I like the thought that goes into bending over a canvas or a potter's wheel—'

'Or a workbench?'

'You still carve?'

A smile touched his lips. 'When I can. Not that I have much time for it these days. Still paint?'

She mimicked his smile. 'When I can. Like you, life has a habit of getting in the way.'

'Other hobbies?'

'I hike on the weekends, run in the week.'

'Me too.'

'You hike?' She looked surprised and quite rightly so.

'Less of the hiking, more of the running. I spend so much time sitting at a laptop or in meetings, getting fresh air when I can escape is important to me.'

'Me too.'

'You hated running when we were kids. You'd never come with me.'

She laughed. 'That's because back then you'd run on a Sunday morning when Maggie was doing her big baking session, and getting first dibs on her shortbread was far more important.'

'Aah, yes, so true.'

'Plus, it gave me some peace and quiet to read.'

He grinned. 'Still a romance lover?'

'Of course.'

'Still after your own happy ever after?'

Her hand stilled as she reached for her wine glass, her eyes hesitant. 'Isn't that why we're here?'

'No,' he bit out, his defences rebuilding so fast he felt something akin to whiplash. 'I've told you why I'm here. I have no intention of marrying and you claim you're here because of your friends, but there was a time...' He eyed her left hand, the finger that had once borne not only his ring but another man's. 'What happened between you and Tim?'

She straightened up, forgetting her wine entirely as she swallowed and eyed him carefully. 'Tim? How did you...?'

The warning bells chimed. He'd given far too much away. Revealing that he knew of her life after him revealed that he'd cared enough to find out. It was stupid, but he could hardly take it back. Seeing her announcement on social media, the happy couple with the hand bearing the ring on show, had been a turning point for him. A reason to look to the future and to accept that she would never be a part of it.

'I used to keep tabs on you.'

'You kept *tabs* on me?'

'What?' He shrugged. 'You never looked me up in this day and age where everyone's business is everybody's thanks to the wonder that is social media?'

'But you're not even on…' She broke off, her cheeks flushing anew. 'Okay, so, yes, I did search for you. But other than the great strides you've made with your charity, your business, which I know has nothing to do with your family and everything to do with you, you're a mystery.'

'My sister more than makes up for my lack of presence in the media—social or otherwise. She's been adept at courting the media ever since she could talk.'

Her smile was slow but filled with affection now. It caught at him even as he acknowledged it wasn't directed at him but his sister.

'How is Ally?'

'Now *that* you must know already.'

She picked up her cutlery, tasted a morsel. 'I'm sure the media don't give the whole truth, though.'

'In this case, they've not gone far wrong. She's well, she's happy and she keeps them away from me, which is just the way I like it.'

Her smile was one of understanding. 'I read she was expecting her second child.'

'She is.'

'So, how does it feel, being an uncle?'

His chest warmed, masking the pang that lay beneath. He was happy for his sister, the marriage she'd been steered towards had been good for her—she'd found love and happiness and in turn had made their parents happy too. 'Much the same. Though it's had me coming home more.'

She seemed to struggle with the portion of food she had taken, swallowing and chasing it down with more wine. 'It has?'

'Yes.' He nodded, trying to understand her reaction. 'I always intended to return eventually.'

'Permanently?' It virtually squeaked out of her.

'Yes. I couldn't stay away for ever. My parents are getting older, the estate still needs managing and though Rupert does an excellent job, he too is getting on.'

'So…the prodigal son returns?'

'Something like that.'

She considered him for a long moment. 'Well, there's another tick in M's box.'

'How so?'

'Edinburgh. It's not just where we're from…' She placed her cutlery together on her plate, signifying she was done, and sat back in her seat, taking her wine with her. 'I take it you mentioned your intention to set up more of a base there in your talk with Madison?'

He frowned, thinking back over his conversation. 'I did. But I thought… Are you saying you live in Edinburgh now? I thought you moved away.'

'I did. I left to study at Warwick University, then moved to London, but my heart was always in Edinburgh. When Mum got sick…'

She stopped, her eyes glistening as she looked away and her hand went to her locket—her mum, that was who was inside it, he should have guessed. And now he felt like an insensitive buffoon for leading them down this path.

'I was sorry to learn of your mum's passing, Jas,' he said softly, hoping that she would believe him and take the apology for what it was, sincere and heartfelt, regardless of their history. 'I wanted to pay my respects and come to the funeral, but…well, by then you had Tim and had obviously moved on. I didn't want to tread on anyone's toes, or…' He waved a hand as words failed him.

'You should have come.'

Her ardent declaration surprised him. 'Why?'

'Mum would have liked it, she always thought highly of you.'

'That wasn't the impression she ever gave me.' He frowned. 'Or you.'

'She just wanted her only child to be happy. She wanted to protect me.'

'And she didn't feel I could do that? I would have done everything in my power to make you happy. Protected you, doted on you, loved you.' He could feel his voice vibrate with vehemence, but this was ancient history, he shouldn't care as deeply as he so obviously did. It shook him up just as much as it so obviously did her. Her eyes were wide, her body still.

'I know you would have,' she said quietly. 'But it wasn't about you, it was about the situation we were in.'

'It was about my family.' He threw it at her, condemning her, because it didn't matter that her reasons had centred on *his* family. At the end of the day *she* was the one who had walked. She was the one who hadn't had faith in him to make it work.

Ten years it had been, and he remembered it like yesterday. The moment he'd turned to her in the great hall, the glass of champagne clutched so tightly in his hand he'd been surprised it hadn't snapped.

'I can't do this, Freddie,' she had pleaded, avoiding the eyes of his disapproving parents beside him, her hand squeezing his as she'd tried to tug him out of centre stage.

'At least one of you is talking sense, son,' his

father had said, uncaring of their audience as his mother had given a high-pitched laugh.

'Yes, dear, you can be so fantastical at times.'

'Fantastical,' he had thrown back at them. 'I'm being nothing of the sort. We're in love and we're getting married, whether you like it or not.'

'Quieten down,' his father had warned through gritted teeth, forcing a smile as he'd waved down their growing audience. 'Do you really want to turn this family into a laughingstock?'

His mother had turned to his father then, her hand gentle on his chest. 'Easy, Alan...'

'Freddie.' Jasmine had tugged on his hand. 'Freddie!'

He'd seen Jasmine's mother amongst the stunned audience, her face ashen, her panicked, fearful eyes on her daughter. How could she not have known that he would love Jasmine for the rest of his days?

He'd smiled then, determined to show them all as he'd raised his glass to the room. 'Ladies and gentlemen, may I introduce you to—' Her hand had slipped from his, killing off his words. She was running away, pushing through the people, her body and head shaking.

'Jas!' He'd run after her, through the double doors, the hall, out into the night.

He'd caught up with her on the stone entrance steps. Fairy lights had adorned the trees and the topiary cones, the festive warmth all the more jarring for her—she'd been ghostlike, her harried breath billowing in the frosty night air as she'd spun to face him.

'Just let me go, Freddie,' she'd begged. 'This will never work. You belong here, I don't. Listen to your parents, they're right.'

'No, Red.' He'd tried to reach for her, but she'd backed away, tugging his ring from her finger, and when he'd refused to take it, she'd placed it on the ground between them.

'I won't give up on us,' he'd told her.

'You have to.' She'd stared up at him, green eyes wide. 'I can't do this, it's over.'

'I think you'd best leave her.' Jasmine's mother had appeared, her hand soft on his shoulder, and he'd gaped at her, his head shaking.

'But I love her.'

'I can't love you, Freddie,' Jas had thrown at him. 'I can't.'

'But you do!'

She hadn't answered, only turned away and run, her mother hot on her tail. She hadn't given him a chance to talk her round, to hold her, to reassure her.

'Freddie?' Jasmine reached across the table, jarring him back to the present and the stinging sensation in his tightly clenched fist as she covered it with her palm. 'It doesn't help, raking over old ground.'

'No, it doesn't.' He unclenched his hand and

pulled it away from her, flexing his fingers to ease the damage his nails had done, not to mention her touch… 'Your mother was the final straw, though. She took you away, she helped convince you I wasn't good enough.'

'No.' She shook her head, her lonely hand going to her wine glass instead, and he wondered if it was her way of hiding how his physical withdrawal hurt. He hoped so.

'All my mother did was tell me everything I already knew. That your family were powerful, influential, and they had their hopes pinned on a high-profile marriage and no matter how much I loved you, I would never be good enough in their eyes. In the eyes of their peers. And that, eventually, it would wear me down.'

'And I would have picked you right back up again.' Why was he even fighting this out now? It didn't matter. It didn't change anything.

'It wasn't that simple, and you know it. You love your family and I couldn't bear to come between you.'

'That was for me to decide, not you.' And there he went again, fighting her on something that should be ancient history. Only now they were together again, airing an age-old argument they'd never had the opportunity to have.

She dragged in a breath, the mood at the table turning dark, haunted by the past, shaken up by the future and the possibility of seven days without the outside world interfering.

'I don't want to argue about this.' She set her wine glass down again, crossed her arms.

'Neither do I.'

'You were the one who said to forget the past, to focus on this week and forget everything else. And yet here we are, focusing on the past.'

Movement off to the right caught his eye. Monique was returning and he sent her a smile before looking back to Jasmine.

'You're right.' She was. And yet still the questions burned through him, demanding answers, demanding closure after so many years. 'Saved by the next course.'

She turned to smile at Monique, her eyes lighting up her face and sucking the very breath from him.

He should have taken the option to jump when she'd given it. Because one thing was for sure, he wasn't as over the past as he'd like to be and what that meant for the next seven days, he didn't know...

But there was no avoiding it. He wasn't running like she once had.

CHAPTER FOUR

'So, YOU LIVE in Edinburgh now?'

Freddie waited for Monique to leave before asking the question and the bubble of relief Jasmine had felt at moving on from the past burst. Because Edinburgh was their past. And her future.

His, too, it now seemed.

She nodded as her stomach turned over and she looked at her plate. The arrangement of food seemed too pretty to eat, she only wished she had the appetite to fully appreciate it.

Living in the same city. No ocean separating them. It was too close. Much too close.

She scooped up some potato confit and popped it in her mouth, her eyes returning to his, and she realised he was waiting for her to expand on the nod. She swallowed, the smooth, creamy potato going down like a boulder.

'I lived with Mum quite a bit towards the end,' she admitted, pain mixing in with the unease. 'And afterwards, when Tim and I split up, I moved back permanently.'

He was concentrating on his plate, dicing up his food. 'He was one of your lecturers at university, wasn't he?'

She dropped her cutlery with a clatter and his eyes lifted to hers with a frown.

'Sorry, I didn't mean it in a negative way.'

'Then why say it at all?' she threw at him. She'd hated that judgement back then and she hated it all the more coming from him now.

'I was...making conversation.'

'Would you like me to quiz you on your exes?'

'Hey, I'm sorry.' He lowered his cutlery and gave her his full attention. 'I didn't mean to upset you. I was just stating a fact.'

'Yes, well, it wasn't like that.' She couldn't calm her voice, or her pulse that raced with the frustrating need to explain herself—she didn't owe him an explanation, yet there she was giving it anyway. 'We didn't date until I graduated. He— he was involved in the launch of my company. He believed in me, gave me the confidence to go after my dreams, helped me secure funding. He was a good man.'

'He was twice your age.' His jaw twitched and she got the impression he was as annoyed with himself for saying it as she was hearing it.

'*And?* We cared for one another, we shared the same interests, and he was passionate about my business venture.'

'As well he should be...' His eyes softened, his mood changing so swiftly she was caught off guard. 'It was a great idea, Jas. Aspirational. Innovative. It had such potential and, of course, it succeeded. I mean, look at you now. I don't know much about your business in recent years, but it's clearly doing well if you can afford the services of M.'

Her chest bloomed with pride, her mouth twitching into a smile she wasn't quite ready to give.

'Yes, it's doing well.'

'So, what happened with Tim?'

'*Seriously*, Freddie?'

'What?' His eyes widened into hers. 'You can't blame me for being curious. The last I knew you were engaged and I…' He shrugged. 'I stopped looking.'

He stopped looking…

She let the confession swirl around her brain, around her heart, her quick-fire anger dissipating in an instant.

'Why were you looking?'

'You really need to ask me that?'

'Okay, why did you *stop* looking?'

'And I repeat, you really need to ask me that?'

He looked away and reached for his glass, but she could see the haunted look in his eyes, could see his answer even if he wouldn't put words to it.

'Tim and I broke up because…'

She stopped. How could she tell him the truth? That on her sick bed her mother had told her not to go through with the marriage, told her it wasn't true love, not like the love that she had shared with Freddie. That if Jasmine searched her heart well enough, she'd know it too. That she was sorry she hadn't backed them all those years ago…

No, she couldn't tell him that.

He sipped at his wine, watched her over the rim of the glass. 'You broke up because…?'

'Because he felt I was married to my job.' It was close enough to the truth.

His lips quirked, his eyes suddenly shone. 'Now, on that I'll raise my glass to you, because there we are one and the same.'

'You too?'

'Haven't I already said I don't have time for a relationship? It wasn't some throwaway remark, it's something that's been proved many times over by the women I date. They get needy, I cut the ties.'

'How very caring of you.'

'Quit the judgement, Jas. I'm always honest and open, maybe brutal at times, but it's as much for their benefit as it is mine.'

'And you're happy living like that?'

'What? Single?'

'Alone?' It sounded sad coming from her lips. It *felt* sad. It didn't matter that she too had proved over the years that her job came first. That anything serious demanded time she couldn't give. Or was it more that she hadn't *wanted* to give that time? That her mother had been right to think true love would have encouraged her to find that balance?

That Freddie would have.

'It's the only way I know how to be.'

His honest declaration sliced through her thoughts, chilling her through. Freddie, alone. It wasn't him. Not the Freddie she'd grown up with, surrounded by his family, her. She wet her lips, started to say something but he got there first.

'So, you broke off the engagement?'

She bristled. She didn't want the focus back on her, but she didn't want the rush of guilt either, the feeling that she was the reason he now stood alone…

'It must have been hard,' he pressed. 'You were together a while.'

'Tim knew it was coming,' she rolled on, trying to shrug it off. 'We'd grown comfortable with one another. We still loved each other, but it was the kind you share with a best friend, not a husband.'

'We were best friends once.'

Her heart pulsed in her chest. 'We were lovers too, Freddie.'

A small smile touched his lips. 'I'll take that as a compliment.'

A compliment?

She frowned as his smile lifted off to one side, his brows rising, and his meaning hit home: he was more of a lover than Tim had ever been.

'All right, Casanova…' she laughed in spite of herself '…get back in your box.'

He laughed too, his eyes drifting to the ocean.

A silence descended, more marked for the laughter that had preceded it. He was lost in the view—and the past, she was sure—and she dreaded whatever was coming next. She searched for something to fill the quiet, anything to get there first...

'So, has there been anyone since?'

She started as he struck at the same nerve, his eyes coming back to her.

'Are we really doing this? Going over our exes?'

He shrugged. 'Why not?'

Because it was the last thing she wanted to discuss.

She didn't want to know about the women that had warmed his bed over the years.

There were sure to be many. A man who looked like Freddie, with his confident and charming aura, would never be short of a willing companion.

'Because it's in the past, remember?'

'I'm just curious. Past aside, it's hard to date in general, but when you have money, it's a different challenge altogether. Wouldn't you agree?'

'Aw, don't tell me little Freddie Highgrove is worried women want him for his money rather than his dashing good looks...' She was trying to deflect, to tease, but instead she'd given more away than she'd intended.

'So, you still think I'm dashing?' His dark smile was dangerous to her libido and she tried not to look at him—tried and failed.

'That wasn't what I meant...' But the blush to her cheeks was confirmation enough and she cursed the colour of her hair for making her so transparent.

'You have to admit money is a problem,' he pressed. 'It's part of the reason M is so successful.'

'True.'

'So, has there?'

She shook her head, exasperated. '*No*, Freddie, as it happens, there's been no one I would call serious. Not since Tim.'

'No one at all?' She didn't like the surprise and disbelief in his wide and far too alluring blue eyes.

'Not everyone needs someone to fill their bed, Freddie. Judging by your reaction, you're not one of those people.'

'Having your bed warmed, as you so put it, is different from a serious relationship, and I'm all for the former.'

She wasn't sure which irked her more. The acknowledgement that Freddie's bed had been well and truly warmed over the years, or his affirmation to stay single. One told her she was jealous, the other told her that a small part of her hoped for an impossible future together.

Both were utterly ridiculous.

She stabbed at her food with gusto, her eyes burning into the plate. Why should it bother her? Any of it? He'd stopped being hers long ago. She shouldn't care. And she hardly had time for a real relationship herself. Didn't the breakdown of her engagement with Tim prove that?

But the fire still blazing inside simply mocked her, his dry chuckle provoking it.

She glared at him. 'What's so funny?'

'You.'

Her breath gusted out of her. There were no words. None at all.

'I may not live the life of a monk…' he took up his cutlery, releasing her from his far too astute and disturbing gaze '…but I never pretend to be after more.'

'Well, bully for you!' She forgot about her food, her appetite going on, off, on, off with their conversation. 'Did you tell Madison you were only looking for a bit of fun?'

His lips twitched with contained laughter as he met her eye for a beat. 'I was honest enough. Now eat. You look like you could do with it.'

His eyes flicked over her again, and this time it wasn't with the raw hunger she'd spied there previously, or with teasing, or anger, it was…concern.

She prickled. 'Don't you start.'

'What?'

'Telling me to eat. My friends get at me enough, I don't need it from you too.'

He gave a small shrug. 'There must be something in it if they're saying it.'

'I've already told you, I run, I exercise, and I am busy. I eat as and when I can. Satisfied?'

She knew she was overreacting, her anger coming from the confusing mess inside. The last thing she needed was for him to send her mixed messages. The one that said they could enjoy seven days and go their separate ways again was fine. It was simple, clear, she knew where she stood.

The one looking at her with concern softening his gaze and making her tummy flutter was not fine.

This one suggested he cared. It confused things, and confusion could only open her heart up to trouble.

'Fair enough.' He didn't quite meet her eyes this time. 'I guess you no longer have easy access to Maggie's baked goodies either.'

She got the distinct impression he hadn't wanted to say it, but it had come out anyway. There was a sadness, a distance to both his voice and eyes.

'No.' She studied his face, desperate to understand where his head had suddenly gone. 'How is Maggie? Does she still cook for your parents?'

'She does.' He took a bite of his food, chewed it. 'She's as much a part of Highgrove as the building itself.'

'She certainly made the place smell heavenly and if I'm honest…' his eyes lifted to hers and she almost kept the rest locked inside, but '… I miss her hugs as much as her shortbread.'

He gave her a small smile. 'I think she'd say the same about you.'

'Except I'm a lousy cook, so cuddles would be her lot.'

The smile was still there, but his eyes were lost in his thoughts, and she opened her mouth to ask for them, but he cleared his throat and looked back at his plate, the moment and the pleasant memories evaporating.

'Anyway, tell me more about your app. What sparked the idea?'

It took a while for her brain to catch up with his rapid switch in focus but her company, her app, were things she could talk about in her sleep and she followed his lead, her smile coming with her words. 'It was actually Mum that gave me the idea.'

Not just Mum, but herself and Freddie too—their inequality due to their start in life—but she wasn't about to tread over that ground again. She hurried on, 'I realised that Mum had an eye for business but not for technology. And, of course, every business needs a web presence in this day and age, and it can be quite a barrier to entry.'

'Indeed.' He was listening intently, and she found she liked it. Liked it a little too much. 'It's a necessary evil in some cases.'

'And it's not just about getting the web presence, but maintaining and updating it, keeping it simple to use. Then there's the financial aspects, billing, accounts and so on. I built an app that would give people like my mum access to all this in one place. Not only does it manage the operational side of things, it gives them a face on the web, a means of advertising their services to garner new clients as well as advertising for vacancies too.'

'Work Made Simple—it's a catchy name too.'

He really had read up on her...

'Again, Mum.' She smiled all the more as she remembered that particular brainstorming session.

'My parents missed her when she left, you know.'

She took a shaky breath, her fingers fluttering over her locket. 'I'm sorry for that.'

'Why are you sorry?'

'Why do you think?'

'It wasn't your...well, all right, but we all had a hand in it.'

She swallowed. So much for steering clear of their past again.

'Anyway, Mum built up a business that contracted out skilled housekeepers, maids, she even had a few butlers on her books by the time...the time...' Her voice cracked and she tried to hurry on, eager not to break down, eager not to feel the pain. 'And then one of those butlers took over the business. It's still doing well now. He's my longest-running client.'

'That's good.' He held her gaze, and she couldn't

breathe for the compassion she could see in his. 'I meant what I said, Jas. She was a good woman. I'm sorry I wasn't there.'

She tried to wave down his sympathy, tried to swallow back the tears and the pain tightening up her throat. And then his hand was there, taking hers, which she was still waving between them.

His fingers, warm and reassuring, pulsed around hers. 'I am sorry.'

She gave him weak smile. 'I know.'

She took a slow breath as she pulled her fingers away from his grasp, the physical connection too tempting to maintain, and took up her cutlery. 'Now we should definitely eat, or this will be stone cold.'

'Of course.' His voice was husky, his eyes still on her. She had the sense there was more he wanted to say, more he wanted to do even, but then he followed her lead.

They kept to safer topics for the rest of the meal, both of them skirting around the past that was never far from rearing up again. The food was delicious, the wines chosen to accompany each of the five courses perfect too. But the more she drank, the more she could feel herself getting lost in his eyes, the more she *wanted* to get lost in those eyes.

'You okay, Jas?'

'Hmm?'

'You're sporting that glow.'

She shook her head, felt the lighthouse spin around her. 'That glow?'

He reached out, his palm soft and warm on her cheek. *Wow, so nice.*

'The one you used to get when you'd had one too many Bacardi Breezers.'

Oh, no. He was right. She wasn't used to drinking. And they'd had a glass with every course, plus the champagne, and that made...that made how many glasses?

'Come on, I'll walk you back to your room.'

'How do you know where my room is?'

'I was given the grand tour before your arrival.'

'Oh...'

He stood and walked around the table, offering his hand to her. She eyed it, wary and wanting to take it all the same. It had felt nice, too nice, to have him hold her hand earlier. The same again when he'd touched her cheek, offering comfort. And now...

She looked up into his face, her smile weak with the runaway thoughts inside her. She slipped her hand into his and lowered her lashes, trying to hide the way the contact made her feel. There was no hiding the flush to her cheeks, though, and she prayed he'd put it all down to the alcohol.

'Thank you.'

She let go as soon as she was standing, her cautious side still capable of taking the driving seat as she sought to put some distance between them.

But it was no use. As they walked, they seemed to get closer and closer. She wasn't sure who was to blame. But as his scent wrapped around her, she felt her entire body thrum with awareness of his.

They reached the head of the steps down to the main house and then she felt his palm soft on her lower back, the light contact working right the way through her.

She didn't dare look up at him, just kept moving, focused on putting one foot in front of the other as he kept his palm there, a connection she didn't want to break.

Her heart pounded in her ears, her breaths coming too fast and too loud. Surely he knew what he was doing to her? Surely he knew how much she wanted to turn into him and kiss him? Kiss him with an abandon she hadn't felt in…in for ever.

She barely noticed the beauty of the garden at night, the swaying palms, the flying fruit bats, the lizards in the undergrowth. She was wholly wrapped up in him and the realisation that she didn't want to go into her room alone.

'Well, we're here.'

'Hmm?'

He gestured to her door, his smile bemused, and she blushed—of course, they were here, she could see that for herself, only…

She looked up at him, her mouth feeling too dry to speak.

'Freddie…' It was barely audible and she wet

her lips to try again, watched as his eyes fell to the movement, darkening with the same fire she could feel building inside.

'Yes, Red.'

A thrill rippled down her spine. 'I don't know what I want to say.'

She knew what she wanted to do, though, and her palms pressed into his chest, almost of their own volition.

'Red…' His muscles contracted beneath her touch, his warmth teasing into her as he bowed his head and she closed her eyes… *Oh, yes.*

But he bypassed her lips and as she opened her eyes, his cheek brushed ever so slightly against her heated flesh.

'It is good to see you again,' he whispered beside her ear as her breath caught. 'Sweet dreams.'

And then he was gone, the moment with it.

Had she imagined it? Had it all been in her head that he'd wanted to kiss her? Was he *teasing* her?

She watched him walk away, pleaded silently with him for one backward glance, just one…

Nothing.

Nothing at all.

And her heart felt it as fresh as it had ten years ago, only then it had been her doing the walking.

Was this to be her punishment now? To have him within reach for a week but his heart unattainable? Her own, on the other hand…

She clenched her fists together and turned away.

She'd just have to make sure she remembered the score, remind herself of it at every opportunity. Freddie would never be hers again, no matter what her reawakened heart was trying to say otherwise.

And it was as it should be.

It had been hard enough to move on ten years ago. To fall in love now when he was so set against marriage, relationships even…

And she had a life in Edinburgh, a successful business that kept her occupied twenty-four seven. She didn't have time for a real relationship either, *Freddie dearest*.

She pushed open her bedroom door, ignoring the voices of Sadie and Izzy in her head, reminding her of why she'd needed M in the first place: to get a life.

A life was one thing. A life with Freddie was something else entirely, and he'd made it very clear it was not, neither would it ever be, an option.

And that was fine with her. She swung her door closed with finality. One hundred percent tickety-boo!

CHAPTER FIVE

'OH, NO, YOU'VE got to be kidding!'

Freddie looked up at the sound of Jasmine's groan and tried to ignore the way his heart lurched at her arrival. And the way the sight of her slight frame still nagged at him. Or was it just that he was so much broader and muscular now that she only *appeared* to be worryingly slender?

'What's wrong?'

Behind her fashionably large shades, she eyed the bicycles he was crouched over.

'Are we *really* doing this today?'

He straightened, chuckling even as he acknowledged how she'd shaken up his trusted composure, his entire life, by turning up here. 'Haven't you looked over the itinerary M prepared?'

'I did. I just…forgot.'

He rubbed the back of his head as he fought the way his body warmed, every degree nothing to do with the midday sun high in the clear blue sky and everything to do with her. 'Are you saying you don't want to cycle?'

'No—no, it's fine.'

She pressed her fingers to her temples and his eyes dipped to take in more of her. She'd swept some gloss over her pink lips. The freckles dusting her nose, her chest, her arms were more prominent in daylight. Her hair too gleamed as it swung freely over her shoulders. The emerald-green vest top she wore was tucked loosely into a pair of cropped white shorts that left too much of her legs on show, their toned and lightly freckled lengths teasing at him.

She blew out a breath and his eyes shot back to her face.

'Feeling a little delicate?'

She raised her chin, her eyes glaring at him, he was sure, and he cursed the tinted barrier between him and her green eyes. He'd missed them. Until last night, he hadn't realised just how much he'd missed them.

'Don't rib me.'

His mouth lifted to one side and he raised his hand, fighting back the urge to laugh. 'I wouldn't dare. It explains why I missed you at breakfast, though.'

Not that he'd *missed* her missed her, because that would be foolish.

Her brow wrinkled with her frown and she pocketed her hands, looking back towards the bright yellow bicycles.

'I wasn't hungry. And it was a long day of travelling yesterday. And sleep wasn't exactly…' She chewed the corner of her mouth and he wondered where her thoughts had gone. Were they with his somewhere in very non-platonic territory?

Or was she simply nervous? She always used

to distract him with her mouth when she was nervous. Much like she had last night. Biting it, chewing it, drawing his attention...*eyes up!*

'Sleep wasn't really forthcoming.'

'Too much wine?' he managed to ask through the tightness in his throat.

'I said don't rib me!'

Her frown deepened and he had to bite back his grin. He did feel for her, especially as she'd paled over his mention of wine.

'Apologies.'

She pressed her palms to her cheeks and sucked in another breath, blew it out slowly.

'Right... I can do this,' she murmured against her hands, turning to scan the deserted pathway and gardens.

Almost every colour of the rainbow was covered in the island's vibrant vegetation and fauna, but there wasn't another human in sight. Her eyes came back to him—slow, unsure—her hands falling to her sides. 'Do we not have a guide for this little escapade? I really don't fancy getting lost in the wilderness.'

He laughed now. He couldn't help it, and it felt good. Different. Lighter without the shock hanging over them. 'You know this island is tiny, right?'

'And you know I can get lost in a shopping centre, right?'

He shook his head, his grin uncontainable. 'You can't still be as bad as all that?'

'Wanna bet?'

He laughed more. 'In that case, I'll lead the way, though...' He looked at her feet, at the dusty pink-tipped toes in the gold leather flip-flops, and felt a ridiculous tightening in his core. Was there anything about her that didn't seem alluring and dainty, calling to his protective instincts as surely as a wounded puppy would? 'You might want to change your footwear.'

She followed his line of sight, fluttered her toes. 'You've got a point. Just give me a wee minute.'

She turned and hurried back in the direction of her room, her behind far too tantalising in the flimsy shorts, and he wished he'd asked M to send them skiing. Not only to avoid the Seychelles but to gain extra layers, lots and lots of extra padding, anything to stop him lusting over her like some lovesick teen.

Like the lovesick teen he'd once been...

He threw his attention into making sure the bikes were solid, safe. Checked and checked again that the two cool bags Monique had given him, containing a picnic lunch, were still snug inside the baskets on the front of the bicycles. And waited.

True to her word, she was quick, swapping her sandals for a pair of trainers and a white cap.

'I'm all yours.'

No sooner had she said it than she coloured, her cheeks clashing with the colour of her hair, and he cleared his throat and tugged his sunglasses out of the chest pocket of his linen shirt. He shoved them on, gaining the same layer of protection to stop her reading him like an open book.

'You have sunscreen on?'

She planted her fists on her hips and tapped her foot. 'Yes, as it happens. Do *you*?'

He chuckled. 'Sorry, force of habit.'

The force of habit that always had him looking out for her, looking after her...but he wasn't so sure this Jas would ever need looking after. Oh, she suffered with the blushes still, but there was a fight to her, a confidence. And he liked it and hated that he liked it.

He kicked the stand up on her bicycle and the thing lurched forward.

'Easy, tiger.' She gave a laugh-cum-snort and he pretended not to notice the curious look she sent him.

'Climb on, the seat should be about right. If not...'

She gripped the handlebars, preparing to hook her leg over. 'This should be fun.'

She clearly didn't mean it.

'Not a fan of cycling?'

'I haven't been on a bike, not one of the non-static variety, since I was in my teens.'

Since they'd been together...

The thought came unbidden, the memories too. Of bike trails and picnics and exploring the grounds of Highgrove and further afield. Happy times. Easy.

He shot it all down and reached out to grip the centre of the bike handlebars, holding it steady for her. The move brought her close, so close that her scent drifted up to him, the power of it all the more forceful without the shock of last night.

Was it her perfume, her shampoo…?

He didn't know, but it was soft, floral with a hint of coconut, and his body stirred to life.

'You know what they say…' He cringed at the hoarseness to his voice. 'You never forget.'

She grumbled something incoherent but very definitely curse-like and he grinned, forgetting his discomfort. 'I can arrange for a buggy if you'd rather explore the island that way?'

'What, and give you the satisfaction of thinking I'm chicken?' She turned to him then, her smile so bright he was imprisoned by it, immobilised, and thanked the heavens that he still had his sunglasses on. 'No way.'

She hooked her leg over, her body forcing his away a little as she planted her feet either side of the bike, went up on tiptoe and nudged the seat with her bum. 'It's good, you can let go now.'

'You sure?'

She pursed her lips and raised her eyebrows above the rim of her shades.

'Okay.' He lifted his hands, palms out in sur-render, and stepped back. 'Off you go then.'

She looked down, kicked a pedal into posi-tion, sending it too far, tried again and had it. She pushed off with a wobbly, 'I've got thi-i-i-s.'

He chuckled after her shaky form, too enter-tained to be ill at ease now.

'You sure you're okay?' he called after her, his grin unstoppable.

The front wheel was going this way and that, her movements stilted and awkward and so very funny.

'I'm fi-i-i-ne.' It undulated out of her as she kept her eyes fixed ahead, her balance steadily return-ing. 'Are you go-going to lead the way before I get us lo-o-st?'

'We're still on the premises, Red!'

'And?'

He laughed, his head shaking as he took hold of his own bike and kicked the stand up. He rode after her, realising the sooner he was in front of her, the sooner he wouldn't need to look at her because the sight of Jasmine riding a bike with all the balance of a toddler was as appealing as seeing her do something as sexy as a lap dance in next to nothing.

Not that she'd ever done such a thing for him, not that she would ever do such a thing in the fu-ture, but now that idea was firmly planted in his brain, he was struggling to think straight.

'You there, Freddie?'

He nodded himself out of his stupor. 'Undertaking on your left.'

'You what, on my...' Her bike veered left just as he came up alongside her and they juddered to a stop. He planted his feet and steadied his bike with his thighs, reaching out to grip her by the waist as he did so.

'Good Lord, Red! Please tell me you know your left from your right.'

Her cheeks flushed as she harrumphed up at him. '*Of course* I know my left from my right, I'm a world-class programmer!'

Not that he could see the relevance of that.

'You just...you just distracted me,' she blustered, her body swelling in his grasp with her sucked-in breath, and he knew he was no longer listening. He was too busy feeling her soft warmth beneath his palms, her breasts pushed up against him and those lips... She'd trapped her bottom lip in her teeth and it was calling to him, nagging at him to tease it from her bite and nip it with his own.

He swallowed back a groan, felt his control seeping through his fingers into her, gifting it to her like he had ten years ago...

'You can let me go now, Freddie.'

She sounded as breathless as he felt and he snapped his hands away, pushed off with his feet and led the way.

He should have looked over his shoulder to check she was following okay, but he couldn't trust himself not to throw the bike down and pull her into his arms. Kiss her like his body so desperately wanted him too.

And if it was just his body demanding it, he'd do just that. It wouldn't matter that it was a brief fling, a bit of fun, he would enjoy it and move on.

But she'd only been back in his life a night... one night, and already those feelings of old were returning. The need to be with her, the joy he found in her smile, in her laugh. All those feelings that pulsed too close to his heart, his heart that had barely survived her ten years ago.

How would he fare now? Ten years older. Ten years wiser. With a multitude of women since and none of them capable of sparking anything close to what she could.

'All right, all right, Freddie!' she called after him. 'You didn't tell me this was some kind of race.'

He grimaced and eased his speed, softly applying the brakes. His fight or flight instinct was clearly kicking in. He looked behind him to see her pedalling faster, steadier, her grin wide. Despite her admonishment, she was having fun. It shone around her in the sun, like an aura that called to him, sucking him in.

Fight or flight?

Right now, he knew which he would choose, and it wasn't the safe and sensible option.

'We *could* have a race.'

She laughed. 'Are you serious?'

'Absolutely.'

'Ever the competitive one, you haven't changed at all.'

'Neither have you.' The soft observation came out automatically and he knew it wasn't quite true. She had changed. And so had he. They'd both grown up, experienced the world, succeeded as far as their corporate dreams were concerned. As for their hearts...

Well, they wouldn't be here now if they'd succeeded there.

And now they were together again...

He shot the thought down as quickly as it sparked.

There would be no second chance.

This wasn't some fairy tale romance, this was reality. And the reality was he had no space in his life for a relationship, not any more. And even if he did, he couldn't trust her to stand by him in the face of his family, he couldn't trust her with his heart again, but he could let go for a week. They could have this time together. Make it as wild and as adventurous as they liked.

'First one to the gatehouse!' she called out, pedalling faster and overtaking him, flashing him an electric grin.

'You're on.'

This truly was paradise and, for whatever reason, they'd been gifted this time together and he wasn't going to waste it getting caught up in feelings he'd long ago shut down.

He was going to make the most of every last wild and adventurous second.

CHAPTER SIX

'I HAVE TO SAY, when I saw the bikes I did think less luxury holiday and more military boot camp,' Jasmine teased as she pressed her hand to her very full stomach and sighed. 'I was wrong.'

'Don't forget, we have a full body massage awaiting us this afternoon. You can see it as earning that little bit of luxury.'

She laughed softly. 'True. And I'm going to need the cycle back just to work off all that food.'

They were lying on a red-chequered picnic blanket under the shade of the gently swaying palms above and the pillowy softness of the white sand beneath. Impressive granite boulders of all shapes and sizes punctuated the coastline, creating a perfect secluded cove.

They truly were in their own private paradise, and what she would give to make things different between them. To rewind ten years...

A sharp squawk from the circling white birds above jarred her out of her reverie and Freddie caught her flinch, his mouth quirking to one side in a gesture that she was swiftly getting used to, her attraction to it much less so.

'Noisy, aren't they?' he said, his eyes on the birds.

'Very. Just like the seagulls back home…though I have to say these are slimmer, more angular.'

'I can't imagine these have ready access to fish and chips.'

She grinned. 'True. And I guess we are intruding on their paradise, they have every right to tell us to do one.'

'What, so they can get at the leftovers from our feast? See, not so different, after all.'

She laughed again and rolled her head to the side, eyeing the spread only half-finished between them. Crusty ciabatta, cheeses, pâtés, pickles and preserves, freshly prepared fruit, homemade nougat and fudge…

He chuckled, his head turning to the side too, his grin touching both corners of his mouth now and flashing his perfect white teeth, the cheeky dimple on the right that reminded her so much of the boy he'd been.

Her heart did a little skip and her eyes flicked to his. They were as blue as his shirt, as endless as the sea and the clear sky above. Their depths ever more captivating and ever more dangerous to her misbehaving body that wanted so desperately to act on his suggestion at dinner the previous night. His suggestion that they '*enjoy*' themselves, indulge in a week of pleasure…

She shivered with the recollection, bit her lip to stop the whimper that wanted to erupt.

He was much less severe today. His smiles were

easier, his body less tense. The change as marked as night to day. But maybe that was it, maybe having the sun shining down on him had lifted the serious aura and made him more like Freddie... *her* Freddie.

And that wasn't a good thing. Freddie looking like his father, reminding her of his father, made it easier to keep some distance between them. But that distance had shrunk with the ease of the day, the fun on the trails, the beauty of their surroundings.

And now as she looked at him she wanted nothing more than to close the physical gap and kiss those lips that looked, oh, so familiar and yet not.

'Jas?'

Scratch the less severe. He looked pensive now. As pensive as she felt, his voice soft and laced with...*lust*?

But she didn't want to get her hopes up, not after last night when he'd left her hanging almost literally.

She looked at the sky, hiding from him. 'Hmm?'

He rolled onto his side, edging that little bit closer, and she kept her eyes up, her palms on her fluttering tummy. This could be it, the moment he would kiss her, the moment they would embark on their six-day fling...

'Do you want some more coconut water?'

She twisted to look at him, her eyes narrowing. 'No. No, I don't want more coconut water.'

I want you.

'Fair enough.' He grinned. Was he doing it on purpose? Drawing it out? Teasing her? Just like he had last night… 'Mind if I finish it?'

'No.' Crumbs, was she going to have to jump him? 'You knock yourself out.'

Her eyes flitted to his hand as he lifted the flask and poured out the remainder, her attention on his fingers, on those tanned lengths that she wanted roaming all over her skin. Old memories merged with new fantasies. He'd been a skilled lover before, thoughtful, attentive, what would he be like now? With all the experience, the added strength to his frame, those shoulders so broad and dominating, she could lose herself against him.

His chuckle pulled her sharply back into reality and she realised she was staring, her lips parted, an expression that could only be interpreted as longing on her face.

'You *sure* you don't want some?'

Eyes on the heavens again, she felt her cheeks burn. 'No, no, I'm good.'

He was still watching her, though. Even as he arched his head back, downing the drink and exposing the long, muscular length of his neck that looked, oh, so very appetising…and now she sounded like some blood-starved vampire!

Eyes to the heavens, Jas.

'That's so good.' He groaned. 'I'm sure it doesn't taste that way back home.'

'Where's home for you now?' she blurted out, desperate for some conversation to beat back her interfering libido. 'Until you return to Edinburgh, that is?'

He lay back on the blanket, his hands behind his head, and she breathed a little easier, even as the chill of disappointment ran through her.

'New York.'

'Will you miss it when you leave?'

He was quiet and she sneaked a peek. Deep in thought, his brows pinched together, he was really thinking about it. 'I don't have time to miss things.'

It was a strange way to put it. But then…didn't she get that? Hadn't Tim accused her of being married to her job, always being on edge when she wasn't at her laptop, tapping out a new programme, identifying opportunities, acting on them. Didn't her friends accuse her of it now?

A man was supposed to change that, but if she was honest with herself, would it really? Maybe she and Freddie had more in common now than ever. And maybe she should be taking his lead and accepting that a relationship, as ideal as it was on paper, just wasn't practical when all was said and done. Not when her heart now belonged to her business. Her business and Freddie from the past…

'If only we could find a way to create more of it.'

'Time?' He grinned at her. 'Your programming skills up to inventing a time machine yet?'

She laughed, a sense of ease building with the realisation that they weren't so different. That Freddie was right to keep it about the week, about the newfound ease they had found, and enjoy it. Not to get hung up on the future…

'I'll be back in New York often enough anyway,' he continued. 'My business and my charity HQ are there, that won't change.'

She thought of all he'd achieved over the last ten years. The amount of effort it must have taken to make something of himself, having broken away from his family. He hadn't taken his family's wealth and survived off it, he'd done his own thing, created his own investment company and his own charity from the ground up. He was as married to his work as she was and as her chest swelled with pride for him, she also acknowledged that he wasn't hers to be proud of any longer.

Her heart was less inclined to agree… But then it was okay to be proud of him, she could still respect him, admire him, *like* him even.

She could still…want him.

She took a steadying breath as her heart raced

with her thoughts and silence stretched between them, broken only by the waves and the wild-life serenading them. A striking red bird fluttered down to peck at a fallen palm leaf an arm's reach away and she smiled.

The pace of life was so very different here, as was the kaleidoscope of colour. Cycling along the shady forest paths, spying all the wildlife going about their daily routines unfazed by the gentle whirring of their bicycle wheels, had been incred-ible. And they'd seen birds of all shapes and sizes, vibrant frogs, geckos…

'I almost feel like we're on a movie set,' she murmured.

A movie set where the man, at any moment, would seduce his willing companion…though there was nothing to say the woman couldn't make the first move.

'It's not called paradise for nothing.'

She sneaked a look at him, the way the mus-cles in his arm flexed as he rested his head on his hands.

'True,' she agreed softly. 'It's perfect.'

'As we always knew it would be.'

He looked at her, his eyes piercing straight through to the sudden pang in her chest, and she looked at the sky again, pulling her sunglasses back down. Thank heavens for oversized shades. She needed the shield just as much now as she had that morning when she'd finally accepted she couldn't hide out in her suite any longer and that she'd have to face him: Freddie. Her perfect match.

She could slap herself silly.

Of course, Madison Morgan and M had chosen Freddie. She'd virtually *asked* for him. His dark hair, his blue eyes, his Scottish roots, his sense of honour, duty, loyalty. His passion for others. His care. His charity efforts.

And had he done the same?

Subconsciously, had he listed all the attributes he'd once loved in her?

M wasn't one-sided, the match depended on the answers he'd given too. And if that was the case, then it didn't matter how married to their work they were, on paper they were as perfect now as—

'You've really made something of yourself, Jas.'

His husky compliment startled her into a choked 'Beg your pardon?'

'You really have.' He grinned in the face of her surprise. 'It's impressive.'

Her heart bloomed under his praise, his smile, pushing out the shock and the uneasy realisation that she cared about his opinion so very much.

'I could say the same about you.'

His brows pinched together. 'Really?'

'Of course,' she said, putting words to what she'd been thinking not minutes before. 'Your charity work is incredible. The strides you've made helping disadvantaged children pursue their dreams…it's something to be commended.'

He shrugged, the movement so dismissive, so small. Did he really not see it that way? And had he been doing the same as her for the past few minutes, thinking over the last ten years and what the other had been doing?

'It's *wonderful*, Freddie.' She said it softly but no less insistently. 'Truly wonderful.'

'I'm not sure I quite see it like that.'

She rose up onto her elbow, stared at him in disbelief. 'How would you see it?'

'My motives aren't so altruistic.' His eyes flicked to her, the slight and very out of place blush to his cheeks telling her he meant it. 'I'd love to say I did it entirely out of the goodness of my heart, but… I don't know, it's not that straight-forward.'

'In what way?'

He was quiet for so long, lost in his thoughts, and she wondered if he would answer at all, but eventually he spoke.

'Sometimes I feel like I'm trying to right a wrong.'

She frowned. 'Why would you think that?'

'Because it's like I'm trying to offset my easy start in life. Offset it by ensuring those who don't have it so easy get the same chances.'

'*And?* That's admirable. It's not something you have to do, it's not your fault, it's not you righting a wrong that *you* have done. You're levelling the playing field of life and *that* is out of the goodness of your heart.'

'Maybe…'

'There's no maybe about it, Freddie.' She needed him to see the good he was doing, she needed him to be proud of it, pleased even.

But there was a strange look in his eyes as they came back to her. 'I can't say I'd be doing it if it wasn't for you.'

'Me?' Her surprise made it more of a gasp.

He nodded, his eyes darkening in their intensity. 'I'm sorry for how my parents treated you, I'm sorry they made you feel like you weren't worthy, I'm sorry they drove you away—'

'No, don't do that. Don't apologise for them.' She shook her head. 'It was me…it was me that left in the end. I just… I just couldn't bear it…'

Her heart was spiralling in her chest, her thoughts so jumbled she couldn't string them into a good enough sentence. The past just wouldn't stay in the past. And the truth was he was perfect just the way he was. The man that loved his family, was loyal to them. To break him away from them ten years ago would have broken that loyalty. It would have broken him.

'It doesn't matter what drove you to set up the charity, Freddie, what matters is that you did.' Her voice vibrated with the pain of old and her desperate need to convey her faith in the man he was now. 'You've helped so many people and have so many success stories under your belt. Your charity has produced sports stars, celebrities, artists, mathematicians, soon-to-be astronauts…'

His mouth twitched. 'You really have been reading up on me.'

Her laugh was soft. She didn't care that she was laying her heart bare just a little, confessing to the fact that she'd never let him go. It was more important that he listened to what she said, absorbed it, acknowledged it for what it was— the truth.

'Those kids stand in the limelight and praise you and your charity for helping them achieve their potential. You must know it in yourself. You must be proud.'

His eyes sparkled, but the shadow of doubt was still there, nagging at her heartstrings, tugging at her breath.

'Carry on like that and I'll be entering my room by the sliding doors at the rear just to get my head inside.'

She knew he was trying to lighten the mood, to take the focus off his accomplishments—to all intents and purposes dismiss them—and she wasn't having it. She touched her hand to his cheek, felt his warmth tease into her palm, felt his jaw flex, his body tense as she encouraged him to hold her eye.

It was the first time she'd touched him so intimately in ten years, ten *long* years, and it made her realise she wanted so much from him. Not just physically but emotionally. It should have scared her off. It should have had her running, but she wouldn't run again, not from him.

'You should be proud of it, Freddie.' She smoothed the pad of her thumb over his cheekbone, marvelling at the chiselled line, the hint of softness and strength. 'You should be pleased with all you've achieved and are continuing to achieve.'

'It's not that I'm not pleased, Red,' he said gruffly. 'And it's not that I'm not proud of the charity and all we've been able to accomplish. It's the lack of fulfilment. It's never enough.'

'But you're driven because you care, that doesn't just go away. There will always be people that need your help and that of the charity.'

'True. But it's the sense that something's missing, like an itch you just can't scratch.'

His eyes strayed over her face, the world around them seemed to slow down, even the noises around them faded.

'Ignore me,' he said softly. 'I'm making no sense.'

'No…' She wet her lips. 'I get it.'

And she did. She knew exactly what he was talking about.

He came up onto his elbow with her. 'You feel it too?'

'The sense that you're still searching for something to make you feel whole?'

He nodded and she returned the gesture, unable to speak, unable to breathe. The air shifted around them, the world falling away completely. He looked at her lips, a small smile playing about his own.

'Crazy, hey?' he murmured. 'Here we are in paradise, money no object, and still we feel unfulfilled.'

Her smile wavered. It wasn't so crazy, not when she thought about it. Not when she acknowledged that the last time she'd felt anywhere near content had been when she'd been in his arms.

But life had been simpler in so many ways then. She'd had Mum, she'd had time for him, she'd had a life…not that she could see a way back to that. Mum was gone now and she had responsibilities, people to help, a company to run…

She could feel him getting closer, or was she leaning in? Her eyes fell to his lips, the appealing fullness to the bottom one, the arch in the centre of the top one…

Yes, Freddie, please, Freddie…

He reached out and anticipation coursed through her, fizzing up her bloodstream, warming her body. His palm smoothed against her cheek, cupped her neck and she tilted her head back, her eyes closing. The first brush of his lips was electric, the sweet sensation all the more powerful for its brevity. A whimper caught in her throat and she leaned closer, seeking more. Another light brush, too delicate, not enough. She parted her lips, angled her head...

'Freddie...' It sighed out of her and she eased closer, let her tongue glide softly against his. *Oh, yes.* And then he was gone, his mouth replaced by his finger as he sealed her lips shut and her breath hitched anew.

'Shh,' he said softly as her eyes flicked open. 'There's a tortoise right behind you.'

Wait, what?

A gulp of air, of disappointment, of humiliation at her wanton state when he was so...*unaffected*?

And then she turned her head and saw just what he was referring to. A giant tortoise was right beside them, bigger than any she had ever seen before.

How had she not sensed it approach?

How? She mentally mocked. *You really need to ask yourself that?*

'He's an Aldabra tortoise.' Freddie was so close she could feel his breath sweep over the delicate skin of her nape, provoking her nerve-endings and the lust still beating fresh in her veins. 'And I'd say he's nearly as big as you.'

'He's incredible.' And he was. But he wasn't the reason she sounded so breathless. No, that was all Freddie.

Undaunted by their presence, the tortoise

paused less than an arm's reach away, his neck straining as he reached ever so slowly for a leaf to munch on.

It was remarkable to watch up close. Like they'd jumped into a TV documentary and any second now the narrator would pipe up: *'And here we see the giant Aldabra tortoise of the Seychelles in its natural habitat and two unsuspecting tourists caught by surprise mid-clinch...'*

The amusing commentary and awe-inspiring sight should have beaten back the emotion swelling inside her, beaten it back and taken over.

Only it didn't…

She wanted Freddie, she wanted his kiss, his body, him…and no amount of paradisal wonder was going to distract her.

No amount of fear over where this was heading either.

CHAPTER SEVEN

SAVED BY A TORTOISE...

It was a new one for him.

But he'd most definitely been saved.

Because that kiss had been a nanosecond away from being way out of his control. Her trapped whimper, her eager response...and he'd been exposed. Raw under her heartfelt praise, lost in the shared sense of dissatisfaction, the acceptance that something was missing for both of them and the merest hint that this could be it.

This could be what they both needed.

Even now, hours later, it hounded him, and he'd been massaged until every limb felt loose. Jasmine too. The masseur and masseuse skilfully ensured every knot was banished as they'd lain beside one another on their separate beds in a cabana high on the granite clifftop. No privacy for more talk, more intimacy.

And it had been a glorious hour, perfect in every way. But no sooner had they stood, their matching bath robes back in place, and he'd looked at her, the high colour in her cheeks, the dreamlike state of those green eyes that he remembered so well, and he was coiled tight again.

They'd walked back to their separate wings in a comfortable silence, but he hadn't missed the way she'd looked at him from beneath her lashes, the smile playing about her lips giving away her thoughts. He'd come so close to pulling her to him and kissing away all sense.

But fear had kept him distant, fear over how much he wanted her.

He wasn't stupid, he'd been able to stay detached from women over the years because he'd never felt an inkling of what he'd felt for Jas. He'd stood alone and had been happy to do so. It had given him the focus he'd needed, the drive to succeed, to keep succeeding.

But this thing with her…it was swelling out of his control. She saw him for who he was, she saw beneath the cool façade, the businessman, the charity organiser. He'd *let* her see beneath it all, confessed his deepest worry, his honest motivation.

He cursed, his fists flexing at his sides.

He needed to keep it within his control if he was to keep his heart out of it, but as he looked towards the beach that was to be the setting for their evening meal and took in the romantic ambience of the scene, he knew he was in trouble.

Monique and her team had excelled themselves. With the sun dipping into the ocean, the scene was already cosy enough, but that was merely a backdrop to what they'd created.

He'd expected a table and chairs, some candles. Instead, there were oversized red cushions, plumped up next to the thick trunk of an aged palm and arranged into a U-shape big enough for the two of them to lounge on. Two copper oil torches were staked into the sand, their fiery glow complemented by tea lights scattered around the ground, their flames protected from the sea breeze by glass domes. A low table housed a copper bowl filled with ice, a bottle of water and champagne already nestled inside. Another table had a selection of glasses and appetisers ready to be devoured.

It was soft, inviting and above all romantic. The perfect scene in which to let go.

No more restraint.

His gut rolled as his flight instinct tried to kick in, telling him to run the other way because the lure of a second chance was getting stronger every second he spent in her company. The idea that maybe he didn't have to go it alone.

He blamed M for being far too good at what they did. Tantalising him with hope, with the belief that this was a second chance. Some quirk of fate with the help of a very clever matchmaking team had brought them back together to make it possible.

But he couldn't believe in it.

He'd been that foolish once to believe in her, in an 'us', and it had ruined him, torn him apart, and it had taken years to let her go.

Correction, it had taken the sight of a ring on her finger to let her go.

But now that ring was long gone.

As was the physical distance between them.

They were very much together, in surroundings geared for a passionate love affair, and he was slowly losing the ability to distinguish between reality and a short-lived fantasy.

He'd been confident, cocky even, to suggest they let go for the time they were here. Put the past in the past and have a wild ride for seven days. Then go back to life as it had been.

Like it would be so easy, so simple.

He'd cursed his younger self for being a fool. What did it make him now as a man whose heart-strings were so readily tugged?

A blasted idiot. A sucker for punishment. An even more desperate fool. And how on earth could he possibly balance a future that was already rammed with his work, his charity pursuits and what would eventually be his inheritance—his title, the land, the Highgrove estate—and all that would demand of him, with the possibility of more?

He could never give Jasmine the attention she would deserve, justifiably demand even. He would be as bad as his father, as bad as—

'Freddie?'

He spun on the spot and lost the ability to breathe. There she was. All he'd been missing for the last ten years as obvious as the feelings clambering back to the surface.

She looked incredible. Her burgundy knee-length dress, hanging from slender straps, twisted across her front, the style and silken surface accentuating every luscious curve. She wore the same locket as the night before and her skin shimmered with whatever product she had applied. As for her hair, it blazed in the setting sun, its kinky undone look softening the angles of her face and making the colour of her eyes all the more striking. The make-up she wore gave them a subtle cat-like slant and he wasn't sure if it was that or the true train of her thoughts that had her looking quite...predatory.

Heat spread through his core as her cheeks flushed pink and she nipped her lip, her fingers lifting to her locket.

She was *nervous*, not predatory. And he was all the things he'd accused himself of being—an idiot, a sucker, a fool!

'Jasmine.' He smiled, hid all of his panic, all of his worry behind it, because the one thing he knew for sure: there was no stopping this. In a week's time, when this was over, he would be free to worry about it as much as he liked...

He offered his hand and she slipped her fingers in his. 'You look amazing, Red.'

Her smile was small, her eyes trailing over him.

Now she looked predatory and it stoked the fire that hadn't quite gone out.

'So do you…' And then she looked at the cushions, the candles, her free hand waving over the entire set-up as she sighed softly. 'And so does this.'

'You going to talk about it being like a movie set again?'

She laughed, walking with him as he led her to the cushions. 'Well, it is.'

'I prefer dreamlike.'

He released her hand as she lowered herself down, her hands sinking into the pillowy softness either side of her as she leaned back and looked up at him. 'Why?'

Because dreamlike meant that he would wake up safe, unaffected, his life wouldn't have changed, his heart wouldn't…

He said nothing. In truth, breathing was proving difficult enough as he took in the sight of her reclined back, her legs curled to the side, a small slit in the dress revealing a tantalising glimpse of thigh, her creamy skin striking against the red of the pillows, her dress, her hair…

He wished he had a camera to capture the moment, to capture it and keep it…*and that was way too sentimental!*

'What is it?' She cocked her head to the side. 'Why are you looking at me like that?'

He tried to swallow past the dryness in his

mouth and shook his head. 'You are stunning, it feels like this backdrop was made for you, made for your unique beauty, your smile, your eyes, your hair.'

Her brows pinched together. 'Have you been drinking already?'

He knew what he sounded like. He knew it because he felt it. Punch drunk. But not from alcohol. From her. All her. His Jasmine. His Red.

Only she wasn't his any more. She had ceased being his ten years ago and by her own choosing. He should be keeping that in mind, using it to protect himself now. Along with the knowledge that by their agreement she *was his*, for six more days, and every cloud...

'Can I not compliment my date when the mood takes me?'

She relaxed back, her smile enchanting. 'Well, when you put it like that...'

'Champagne?'

He needed something to do with his freed hands before he hunched down beside her and pulled her to him and whispered all the sweet nothings that were searing his brain, his heart. Each too loving, too real, and far from temporary.

'Please.'

He lifted the champagne out of the ice, throwing his concentration into unwrapping the foil.

'So-o-o,' she drawled, 'why a dream?'

He studied the metal holding the cork in place,

started to unravel it as he gave her enough of the truth. 'Because a dream feels so very real, despite the fact it's temporary, that when you wake up it's over and there's no going back.'

He looked at her, his eyes delivering the message he needed to not only believe in himself but needed her to understand too. He gripped the cork and twisted the bottle. It released, its pop filling the silence that felt far too heavy thanks to his explanation. Silently, he cursed. He didn't want to ruin the moment. He wanted them focusing on what they had now.

'We can enjoy it while we're in it, though.' He smiled and placed the detritus on the table next to the glasses and took up a flute. 'I propose a toast…'

He filled the glass and offered it to her, forcing himself to hold her eye with confidence and positivity. She took it from him, her smile and eyes both curious.

'Another toast—are you incapable of drinking fizz without one?'

He knew she was referring to his toast the previous evening. How had he phrased it, a toast to their cruel twist of fate? He forced back the rising tide within him and poured a glass for himself. 'Are you objecting to another?'

'Not at all.'

'Good.' He placed the bottle back in its bed of ice and lifted his glass to her. 'To our dream.'

Her lashes fluttered, her eyes shone with…with sadness, and he felt winded.

'Our dream…' she whispered, shaking her hair out a little as she lifted her chin. 'And then we move on.'

'And then we move on,' he repeated.

Because moving on was the right thing to do. He clinked his glass to hers, threw back a gulp… but if it was so right, why did it feel so wrong?

She lowered her gaze, releasing him from its pull as she stroked the cushion beside her. 'Are you going to join me?'

He sat where her hand had been. Hunched forward, his elbows on his knees, his gaze lost in the bubbles rising in his glass, the gold of the drink enhanced by the flickering light of the lanterns and the tea lights.

'Do you wish it had been someone else M had matched you with?' She leaned towards him, her arm brushing against his, the directness of her question so unlike the Red of their youth. Younger Red would have shied away from it and he would have had to press and press until she'd had no choice but to give up the question that was on her mind. Not this Red, though. Not the one that had gained in confidence over the years and built a company from the ground up, a mover and shaker in the tech world, an entrepreneur with both brains and looks and who still had the very kind heart that he'd fallen for.

'I mean, I *know* you came without the true intent of finding love,' she carried on, unaware of the emotional rollercoaster underway inside him. Or maybe she was aware and pressed on anyway. 'But now that you know M is so good at what they do, wouldn't you have liked to meet the person they would have picked if I'd not been on their books?'

'No.' He didn't need to think about it. He turned to look at her, really look at her. 'It doesn't matter what my intent had been when I came here, I am happy to see you Jas. I'm more than happy. M couldn't have called it any better.'

A smile flickered on her lips. 'Your parents will have a hissy fit.'

He grimaced. 'Please, can we not talk about them?'

'You were the one that said this week away was to pacify them, convince them that you were hunting for an appropriate bride. If they find out that M threw me in your path...' She turned away, sipped at her champagne. 'What will you tell them?'

'The truth.'

Her head snapped round, her eyes wide. 'Are you serious?'

'Of course I am. I didn't care what they thought then, and I couldn't care less now.'

Her eyes blazed. 'Don't say that, Freddie. You *do* care, you *always* cared. And so you should.

They're your mum and dad, they only want what's best for you.'

'And what *I* want is what's best for me. I told you that then, and I'm telling you again now.'

He watched her drag in a shaky breath, watched the emotions passing rapidly over her face, and he couldn't bear it any more. Having her so close and not...

He reached forward, his hand sinking into her hair as he held her close.

'And what I want right now, is you, Red.' He looked into her eyes and leaned in, any sign, any rejection and he would have stopped. 'I want you.'

She tilted her head back, her lips parting softly. 'You do?'

'I do.'

And then he was there, capturing her mouth with his, the contact lighting up his core. She tasted of champagne. Champagne and something else. Something that was all her. He groaned as he lost himself in it, heard her own little whimper through the blood pounding in his ears. She forked a hand through his hair and clung to him, deepening the kiss.

It was everything and not enough at once, the heat consuming him, driving him to want so much more, regardless of their surroundings and the champagne flutes still clutched in their hands.

He broke away, pressed his forehead to hers as he sucked in a breath.

'I want you, Red.' He was repeating himself, but he couldn't stop the words from tumbling out. 'Tell me that you want me too?'

'More than anything.' He saw the assurance in her eyes, heard it in her breathless words. He closed his eyes, let it sink in, felt its warmth surround his heart, fill his head. 'Tonight? Come back to my room after dinner?'

She nodded, bit into her lip.

'You will?'

'Yes, Freddie.'

He pulled back before he went too far, before his body took over and he took all that she was offering in her gaze. Because although they were cocooned by the line of palms and luscious vegetation, their sounds masked by the wildlife, he knew Monique and her team would be along to check on them shortly.

'Appetiser?' He reached out for the loaded tray and offered it to her, knowing full well nothing would beat the taste of her.

She picked one up, her eyes fixed on him and full of spark. 'I know what I'd rather be tasting…'

She parted her lips and slipped the delicacy inside, drawing the entire movement out, and he gritted his teeth against the lustful heat that threatened to have him throwing both the tray and his caution to the wind.

'You've become impatient in your old age.'

She swallowed, her smile one of absolute tease. 'Says you.'

He grinned. Red of old wouldn't have flirted with him so brazenly either, but he found the confidence of her now even more tantalising than the veiled flirtation of before.

And it should have had the alarm bells ringing ever louder, ever clearer, only they were dull, drowned out by the thud of lust in his bloodstream and the all-consuming rush for her.

Jas. Jasmine. Red.

All her.

Now he wished Monique and her discreet staff would hurry up and disappear again because he wasn't so sure he wanted to wait until they got back to his room…

Red, lying back on the cushions, bare to the moon and his gaze, was far too tantalising an image to resist.

CHAPTER EIGHT

JASMINE *THOUGHT* THE food was delicious. It had to be. A place as exclusive as this wouldn't dare serve anything less, but...

She hardly tasted it. Everything about her was attuned to him. His scent, his presence, the sight of his throat bobbing as he swallowed, the muscles in his forearms flexing each time he reached across her...like he was doing right now.

He took up the bottle of dessert wine and offered to top up her glass.

She nodded, her voice disappearing with the moisture in her mouth. She wanted to kiss him again and the way his eyes kept connecting with hers it was clear she wasn't alone in her desire. His eyes were as dark as the night, projecting such fire, and her insides were molten with it, her limbs taut with growing need.

She sipped at the glass he'd refilled, but really she wanted to be sipping from his lips. The taste he'd given, the sampling of his mouth against hers had been far too brief and far too wicked. The slight graze of his tongue against hers, the way his body had trembled and her own had come alive... Now all she could do was press her thighs together to nurse the budding ache and wish away the rest of the food so she could feast on him.

'Are you no longer hungry?'

She gave a small smile, a shake of the head. If she'd still been high on their kiss, confident with it, she'd tell him exactly what she was hungry for.

'Not even for the last strawberry?' He picked it up and raised it between them.

Her smile grew. She didn't care how clichéd it was, whether he'd meant the offering innocently or not, she was using it to take what she truly wanted. Him.

She placed her glass down and leaned into him on one palm, her free hand coming up to gently clasp his wrist. She pulled him closer, held his eyes as she did so.

'Now, that's an offer I can't refuse.'

She surrounded the plump ripe fruit with her lips, purposefully brushing them against the tips of his fingers. She savoured the sensation, caught how his eyes flared and his lips parted. Her smile was one of both satisfaction and tease as she bit off a piece and devoured it. Freddie plus strawberry...a *true* taste explosion.

'Nice?' It rasped out of him, filled with the very lust she was struggling to keep at bay.

'Very.'

His grin was slow, his eyes heated as they watched her mouth. 'Would you like the rest of it?'

Her stomach clenched tightly as she nodded. There was only one way to get the rest... She surrounded his fingers with her lips and dragged her teeth along them, taking the sweet, ripe fruit with her. She pressed a kiss to his fingertips as her mouth closed around it.

'I think Monique and her team are long gone for the evening.' He was so very close now, his scent wrapping around her, engulfing her, drawing her in. 'What do you think?'

All she was thinking was how much she wanted him to kiss her…how much she wanted to kiss him…

She swallowed and subtly licked her lips. 'Yes, I think they're leaving us to it.'

He reached out, his fingers soft in her hair, caressing the sensitive skin of her scalp, and she smiled, her head rolling back into his touch. 'You always knew just how to touch me.'

She didn't care about the many wondrous and varied ways he could take that statement, because every debauched one of them was true.

'Is that so?'

She hummed her agreement as he encouraged her closer.

'Care to elaborate?' he whispered against her mouth, anticipation making her entire body tremble.

She gave a soft laugh. 'The way you would toy with my hair…the way you would kiss my neck, my collarbone, my…' her breath hitched a little '…breasts.'

He inhaled sharply, his nose flaring. Her boldness had surprised him—*good*.

'What else?' he rasped.

She reached out to fork her hands through his hair. It was time to show him more of that boldness, more of the woman she was now.

'The way your fingers would play over my skin while your teeth would nip.' She brushed her nose very lightly against his, let her lashes fall. 'The way you kissed my lips like you wanted to reach every part of me, like you wanted to possess me, brand me...claim me.'

He growled low in his throat and tugged her to him, his lips crushing hers. Hard and demanding. Making up for the last ten years of absence and she was delirious on it. The force of it, the desperate pressure of his mouth, of hers.

She shifted her body closer, dragged him back with her as she dropped to the cushions, forcing him to cover her.

He shook his head, broke the kiss. 'I'll crush you...'

He tried to take his weight onto his elbows, and she tugged him back against her. 'You won't.' She wanted to feel all of him, top to toe. His hot, hard heat covering her own. 'I want you, *all* of you.'

'You have no idea how it feels to hear you say that.' Both his body and his words shook with his sincerity and hope fluttered alive deep inside her, the hope for a future, the kind of hope that could destroy her if she let it in.

She tried to stamp it out, to laugh it off. 'You've been working on your platitudes.'

'I've had years to perfect them.'

An icy shard pierced her heart, a stab of jealousy towards the faceless women over the years. She clutched at it like a life raft, used it keep her afloat and hope at bay. Threw her focus into his mouth, his body, his touch.

He traced hot kisses from her mouth to her ear, flicking her lobe with his tongue, scraping it with his teeth. 'How I missed you, Red.'

His words teased along her ear canal straight to her heart, straight to the hope she was trying so hard to suppress. That they could find a way to make it work, to be together and have all they had achieved…

She gripped his head closer, bit into her lip as his teeth nipped the sensitive pulse point at her throat, and she arched into him.

'I missed you too.' It rasped out of her, broken up by her desire, choked up by her fear. She hooked her legs around his, holding him to her. She never wanted to let him go.

He groaned as his straining erection pulsed against the very heart of her, delivering pressure to the small cluster of nerves begging for his touch, and she moved against him, desperate, her own cry telling him she needed more. His mouth was back on hers, fierce, eager. She rolled her hips, and he pressed against her, a rhythm that she dictated, working her desire to fever pitch and taking him right along with her.

He sucked in a ragged breath, lifted his head to look down into her eyes, his own filled with something akin to wonder. He looked so incredibly sexy. All mussed up by her hands, his cheeks streaked with colour.

'I want to taste all of you, Red. I want to remember every inch of you.' He rested his elbow into the pillow, gazing down at her as he stroked her hair back from her face. 'I want to learn what's changed and what has stayed the same.'

He lowered his hand to the locket around her neck, a sudden shadow falling over his features, and an overwhelming sadness clawed at her throat. No. She didn't want his focus there. On the past. On Mum. She didn't want to remember how he hadn't been there. How she hadn't been able to go to him. To lean on him. And, oh, how she'd wanted to.

'*Kiss me*, Freddie.' Her desperate plea called his attention back to her face. A second's hesitation and then he was there, kissing her with the same desperation she felt inside. The desperation to be rid of the past, the pain, to be consumed by the present.

She clawed at his shirt, raking it up his back, tugging until their kiss prevented it from going any further and he leaned back. She ripped it off, threw it aside before bringing her palms back against him. His chest contracted under her touch and she marvelled at his heat, his strength, both her fingers and eyes taking in every ridge as she clamped her bottom lip in her teeth. And then he was there, nudging her head back, replacing her teeth with his, a sharp tug. Punishing. Carnal.

'You're driving me crazy, Red.'

She raked her nails down his back in answer, arching her body and feeling his heat scorch her breasts through the light fabric of her dress. She wanted it gone, she wanted no more barriers between them, and even as she thought it, she knew it wasn't just the physical barriers she wanted gone. It was the wall around his heart—she wanted it to crumble just like her own, against all of her better judgement. She whimpered, both pleasure and pain forcing the noise to the surface, and he broke away from her lips, dragged kisses along her angled jaw, her arching neck and down further, his fingers easing beneath one skinny strap of her dress.

He slipped it over her shoulder, down her arm, the slowness of the move at odds with the dizzying caress of his tongue, his teeth. Goosebumps erupted over her skin, her nipples straining against her dress, no bra to impede the friction as he ran it lower. She held her breath, heat rushing to every extremity, and choked on a whimper as he exposed one tingling peak. She lowered her gaze, watched as he dropped a kiss to the curve of her breast, the edge of her nipple and then...

She hissed in a breath, bucked as his mouth surrounded her, taking her in deep. She clawed at his hair, cried to the heavens. He was ravenous, his tongue flicking over her, his teeth grazing, a crazy combination that had her writhing and begging and desperate for more.

Her cries clashed with those of the wildlife, the waves, his deep and hungry growl. He slipped his fingers beneath the other strap, faster this time as he lowered the fabric to her waist and reared up. His eyes, dark and carnal, seared her skin as they travelled her length.

She wanted to beg him, plead with him not to stop... She wriggled her hips, closed her thighs around his, telling him with her body what she wanted.

'Please, Freddie!'

'It's been ten years, Red, I'm not rushing this. Seeing you like this, your hair splayed out like a halo, your skin so creamy soft against the red of the pillows.' He dragged in a breath, his body straining above her. 'Let me have this.'

He fisted his hand in the skirt of her dress and gently tugged. 'Let me see you.'

'What if someone comes?'

'They won't. The beach is ours for the evening.'

'How can you know?'

'Trust me, I know.'

He was so certain, so sure, and she did trust him. She trusted him more than she knew was safe. But the time for reservations was long gone. She lifted her lower body, granting him permission to take her dress away, and then she was laid bare. Not just physically, her lace thong concealing nothing, but mentally. Her desires, her wants, her heart...it was all there in her face. There would be time for regrets later, much later...

She bit into her lip, wanted to cover her eyes like it would in some way help, but instead she clamped them shut.

'Red?' His voice was a husky plea. 'Look at me.'

Slowly, she did as he asked, felt the colour burning her cheeks in the face of his impassioned smile. 'You are beautiful, let me worship you like your body deserves.'

She knew he'd misread her hesitation and was thankful for it. She didn't want her emotions getting in the way of this. She wanted to forget them, and he had the power to take them away. Temporarily at least.

She reached out and stroked his cheek, nodded her willingness and brought his head down to hers, kissed him with all the passion still swirling inside. She tried to angle her breasts into his chest, desperate for more friction, and he pulled back.

'Patience.' He brought his hand between them

to trace circles over her skin, teasing at her puckered nipples, her navel, the tip of her thong.

'Freddie…' Her body pulsed into him and his fingers answered her plea, dipping inside the lace, parting her to circle over where she ached the most. Her eyes flared open, caught his looking back at her intently, drinking in her every response.

He almost looked like he loved her. She could almost believe that he loved her. And her heart bloomed in her chest, the warmth spreading out from her core with the spiralling tension. She tried to reach between them, to take him in her hand, to give him the same pleasure he was so readily giving her, and he shook his head.

'No, Red.'

It was gruff, determined, and she hesitated, her frown telling him how she felt as she panted with her mounting climax. She wouldn't last much longer, and she wanted him with her. She wanted him inside her, but…

'I have no protection here,' he whispered, sensing her continued hesitation. He kissed her deeply, his fingers keeping up their dizzying caress.

'But I can still…' she said against his lips.

'There's no rush, we have all night, and right now I have other ideas and every one of them involves pleasuring you.'

Her entire body shuddered with the promise of

it all, the wave of heat so strong it pushed her to the precipice.

'Freddie, I can't—I can't…' She clutched his body to her, her nails clawing into the taut muscles of his back, and she cried out into the night. She was gone, wave after wave racking her body as pleasure akin to that which he had delivered so many years before consumed her. And even then it hadn't felt as all-consuming as this.

He wrapped his arm beneath her, held her against him tightly until the rocking of her body dissipated and she was spent. He kissed her. So deeply and so thoroughly she thought she might expire from lack of oxygen.

But expiring like this…with Freddie so hard and desperate for her…was a fate she would readily face. Because she truly was in paradise, and paradise was where she wanted to stay…as long as he was by her side.

The bedroom spun, his heart pounded, and he knew panic was setting in. Because outside he'd given her his all, had felt her come apart under his touch, his kiss, and he was already addicted to it. The need to pleasure her, to please her, to make her cry out his name, again and again. To cling to him and not let go.

And now she was in his bed, naked and waiting. The locket, glinting in the low light of the room as it nestled between her breasts, exactly where he wanted to be.

Only he wasn't. And why?

Because he was losing it. His control. His grip on reality. On what this was, and what it very much wasn't.

His entire body pulsed with his need for her. Ten years and he hadn't wanted a woman as much as he did her. And he feared that giving in to it would not only strip him of his restraint but his last barrier against her, that this would tip him over from what was safe, what was manageable, into so much more.

But it had been his idea that they do this. Let go for a week and walk away satisfied, the past laid to rest, the future no different.

He'd been a fool, a blind fool. He hadn't seen their connection for what it was, unstoppable, overpowering, impossible to resist. Barely twenty-four hours in, and he was as caught in her unique web as he'd ever been, unable to escape.

'Are you going to stand there all night?' She rolled onto her side, her palm smoothing over the space next to her, the space he should be filling.

'No.' He stalked towards her, breathed deep to get a handle on the heat within and lay down beside her. Took in her entirety stretched out beside him, her skin blushing from where he'd touched her, caressed her, kissed her... He reached out, his fingers gentle on her hip as he caressed the diamond-shaped scar there. Take it slow…just take it slow. 'I remember when you got this.'

She hooked her hands around his neck. 'Well, you should do, since you rescued me.'

'Hardly.'

'I could have been devoured by the Highgrove dogs if not for you.'

He grimaced as he pulled her naked body up against his own, breathed in the fresh scent of her hair and let the memory take over, soothe his core, calm his pulse. 'Well, if you will go scaling walls in desperation to see your lover…'

She nudged her body against him. 'Well, if you will live in heavily guarded fortresses…'

Now he laughed, the sound hearty and earnest and erupting far more frequently than he was used to. His easy grin too. He couldn't remember the last time his cheeks had ached from it, like they did now.

He buried his head into her neck and she laughed, wriggling as the move tickled her sweet spot.

'I missed that sound too.' It was out before he could stop it. The sentiment, the meaning, and she stilled, her fingers soft in his hair.

'Make love to me, then.' She urged his head up to look into his eyes. 'Make me forget those ten years apart existed.'

If only…

He wanted nothing more than to do the same.

To forget. To pretend that they'd moved seamlessly from their teenage love affair to now, where they were much older, much wiser and better prepared for reality. Only…

He needed those ten years, he needed the fateful night she'd left him, to remember this wasn't suddenly going to work out. They had different lives to lead, responsibilities that filled not only their weekday hours but their evenings and weekends too. He wasn't blind to the fact that she worked as hard as he did. Even if her failed relationship with Tim hadn't made that clear, her friends encouraging her on this crazy M date told him plenty.

He kissed her, pushing out the voice of reason as he shucked the rest of his clothes, not once leaving her lips as she helped him.

'You know,' she murmured against his mouth, 'it's lucky no one saw you carrying me back to your room like this.'

'I think if they had they wouldn't have let on.'

'Oh, goodness, I hope not.' She leaned back, looked up at him, wide-eyed. 'Do you think…?'

'Shh…' He bowed his head, pressed his lips to hers. 'If they had, they would only have been pleased that their efforts were paying off.'

She laughed and he treasured the sound all the more.

'You are so beautiful, Red.'

'You need to stop with the platitudes, or else

it'll be me struggling to get my head back into my room later.'

He kissed her. 'Why would you need your room again?'

She laughed all the more, rubbing her nose against his. 'Are you inviting me to stay in your room for the rest of our stay?'

'That depends. Are you accepting?'

She hooked her hands behind his neck and looked up into his eyes. A long drawn-out moment when he doubted everything and hoped for everything all the same.

'Yes.'

He didn't dwell on how her agreement made him feel.

'Good.'

He kissed her again, purposefully losing his mind in her as he reached out blindly for the protection in his bedside drawer. Wishing it could protect him from so much more. He kept kissing her as he rolled it over himself, closed his eyes to push out the look in hers. There was so much going on there, so much emotion, so much...*love*?

But it couldn't be. They couldn't go there. Not again.

'Freddie?' She pushed her hands through his hair, broke their kiss until he opened his eyes. 'What is it? What are you thinking?'

'Nothing, Red.' He shook his head, positioned

himself between her legs as she wrapped them around him. 'Nothing's more important than this.'

Now he held her eye, stared down into her endless greens and asked the question that needed to be voiced, even though he knew the answer well enough, could see it in her eyes, feel it in the way she tried to encourage him against her. 'Are you sure you want this?'

She stared up at him. 'How can you doubt it?'

He didn't doubt it for a second, but he wanted to hear her say it. Didn't matter that she already had, he wanted to hear it from her lips again.

'I want you, Freddie.' She kept her eyes open and pressed a kiss to his lips. 'If I'm honest, you're the only man I've ever truly wanted.'

She sounded so sincere, so much braver than him, and his heart pulsed in his chest, fire coursing through his veins as a long-forgotten possessive streak sprang to life and he couldn't hold back any more. He sank himself inside her, his eyes locked on hers, and she clenched around him, taking his all.

His chest tightened. It was too much, the sense of coming home, of being where he belonged. He shut his eyes, moved inside her, tried to override it all with lust.

Sex was simple. It was just sex. They were where they wanted to be, where they needed to be at that moment.

She clawed at his hair, whimpered and rocked,

his name leaving her with every panted breath, and he couldn't keep his eyes closed any more. He had to drink her in. Her flushed cheeks, her glazed eyes, her every endearment pushing him higher and higher.

'Red, Red, my Red!' It burst from him in a growl as ecstasy claimed him, sheer bliss shuddering through every limb and she tightened around him, her cry drowning out his own.

Her body pulsed, her legs and arms locking him against her. He collapsed, shaken to the very core, his breaths ragged and merging with hers.

Silence descended, their breathing slowed, her grip around him relaxing as her fingertips stroked against his skin, teasing at the goosebumps fresh in the aftermath.

'Wow... Freddie,' she murmured into his throat. 'That was something else.'

He couldn't even look at her, fear of what she would see holding him back. He kept his head over her shoulder, his forehead pressed into the pillow, their combined scent filling up his senses.

How could he get enough of her?

One deep breath.

There were five nights remaining. Could he really have his fill and let her go?

Another breath.

Could he really continue this and leave in one piece?

'Freddie?'

He didn't move.

'Freddie?'

Slowly, he lifted his head, tried to make himself immune, but her eyes…they shone, the golden light of his bedside lamp dancing in their emerald warmth and sucking him in.

He took another breath, rolled onto his back and looked to the ceiling as he pulled her to him. *Chicken.*

'Yes?' he said over the mental gibe.

'Do you think—?' She broke off, her fingers trailing over his chest as she disappeared into her thoughts, but the damage was done, he had to know the rest.

'Do I think…?' He looked down at the top of her head, her blazing red hair all tangled by his hand, and lifted a finger to her chin, titled her head back to look at him.

It was a bad move. Her hesitant green eyes tugged at him, chewed him up inside, but curiosity overrode caution.

And then she blinked, shook her head as she lowered her gaze. 'Doesn't matter.'

His gut twisted—a crazy mix of disappointment and relief.

Whatever she'd been about to say had run deep. Deep with the kind of feelings he was trying hard to avoid. He covered her fingers on his chest, stilling her caress and shutting down the inner torrent. 'We should get some sleep, it will be a busy day tomorrow.'

'It will?'

'You really didn't read the folder M prepared, did you?'

'I did, I just— I keep forgetting.'

'You never used to be this forgetful.'

She gave a small shrug, snuggled in closer to his side. 'You never used to be this distracting.'

And just like that the mood lifted. 'I don't know if I should be flattered or let the younger me be offended.'

'Flattered, definitely flattered.' She pressed a kiss to his pec, her fingers circling over his chest once more. 'So, remind me, what's the plan for tomorrow?'

'We're kayaking in the morning, followed by an evening of cooking the creole way.'

'Couples kayaking and cooking. M really know how to keep you together as much as possible.'

'Is that you saying you're tired of my company already?'

'No. Never.'

His lips curved up, her ardent confession warming him through…until he remembered why that was a very bad sign.

A very bad sign indeed.

CHAPTER NINE

KAYAKING WAS MORE than an adventure activity, it was a scenic delight, the transparent kayaks making not only above sea level a sight to behold, but also below. And with Freddie right behind her, sharing the same kayak, it was a good job too, because she wasn't just distracted by Freddie, she was hooked on him. Dangerously, irresistibly so.

No amount of entertaining chatter from their tour guide and instructor could hold her attention. Each time she turned her head and caught him in her peripheral vision, her body reacted with a fresh wave of heat. Just a glimpse of his skilled hands at the paddles or the broad, muscular expanse of his chest in the tight-fitting blue rash guard that he wore set her off.

And that was before she even got to his grin, or his cerulean eyes, not to mention the sound of his voice, so close… They all just served as a reminder that he was a lover like no other…

A lover like no other? Really, Jas—poetry?

She wanted to roll her eyes, give herself a slap, anything to wake herself up from this Freddie-induced stupor.

'Leaving me to do all the hard work, hey?'

There went his voice again, making her smile and freak out in one, because he was the reason she'd stopped paddling. He was the reason her hands had gone limp around the paddles as she threw her all into getting a grip on her heart.

Her heart that was getting too carried away with every second that passed.

'As it happens...' she angled her head to *almost* eye him, forced a grin as she kept her voice light and breezy '... I'm giving you the opportunity to wow me with your strength and prowess.'

He chuckled, her body getting high on the deep, reverberating sound as she clamped her thighs together and fixed her grin in place.

'I thought I did that last night.'

'Freddie!' She startled, her eyes darting to their guide, Philippe, who wasn't that far ahead in his own kayak.

'You weren't half as bashful last night.'

A laugh erupted from her, her body dizzy with the recollection, dizzy with him.

'Just speaking the truth, Red.'

'We stop here!' Philippe called back, preventing any response she could have thought to give, not that any clear thought existed above the racing of her pulse.

She tugged her eyes from Freddie to see Philippe waving to a section of beach that encapsulated all she had come to love about the island. The luscious greenery sprouting between the granite boulders, the perfect white sand disappearing into the vibrant turquoise sea. Stunning didn't even come close.

'Now I'll show you something really special,' Philippe said as they tugged their kayaks up the beach and straightened.

Philippe's grin was wide, his deep brown eyes sparkling against his bronzed skin as he slung a bag across his back and turned away. He was heading back inland, into a dense stretch of rainforest that she and Freddie had only skirted around on their bikes the day before. It hadn't looked passable with its steep incline and the low-growing plants at the base of the palms. Was he taking them on a hike? In the *midday sun*?

At least with the bikes they had generated a re-freshing breeze to keep their skin dry. After being in the sea and on the kayaks her salt-caked skin felt more in need of a shower than a hike.

'Come. Come.' He gestured and Freddie over-took her, grabbing her hand as he went and shoot-ing sparks of delight right through her.

'Slowcoach.'

'I'm coming,' she returned, a smile teasing at her lips as she shook her head at the back of his.

Yes, Freddie was all man now, but over the last three days, the excitement, the spark of his youth had started to return. The same carefree spark he'd possessed before their relationship had evolved and his parents had learned of it...

Less of the past, Jas! She shoved away the melancholy descending with the thought. *Remember you're living for the now.*

She raced after him, struggling as her feet sank into the sand.

'We'll lose him if we're not careful,' Freddie murmured as Philippe disappeared into the thick vegetation.

'I seriously hope we're not hiking.'

'Don't worry, it's not far,' came Philippe's disembodied voice. 'It's just along this trail.'

Freddie shoved the low-hanging fronds from a palm aside to pull her through and Jasmine frowned at the sight ahead.

What trail?

All she could see were plants, new growth mixing with old as the fallen palm fronds lay dry and crisp along the ground, colour sprouting up in between.

'Come. Come.' Philippe called again, clambering up the sharp incline straight ahead, most of his body disappearing into the trees, and that was when she heard it, the sound of rushing water.

They hurried after him, the excited trill of the wild birds building with the rush of the water.

'Et voilà!' Philippe declared, his arms outstretched in a clearing that took her breath away.

She stilled, Freddie too.

'Wow.' She stared, open-mouthed. It looked like a mirage. A tiny oasis dominated by the palms all around, cut off from the world as the waterfall above their heads fed a small blue lagoon. It was like seeing paradise for the first time all over again. 'I hadn't expected this.'

'You and me both,' Freddie said, squeezing her hand, his one-sided smile just as awestruck.

'You like?' Philippe asked, turning to beam at them.

'Very much so,' she said.

'You can swim here, the water is a little cold, but fresh and good. Deep too, so be careful.' He dumped the bag he'd been carrying on the rock beneath his feet. 'There are refreshments and towels in the bag, and I will go get a coconut.'

He was already off, traipsing back into the forest.

She smiled at Freddie. 'Do you think he's literally going to pick a coconut?'

'I'd say so.'

She shook her head, looking from him to the vision before them, and felt the slick layer of sweat and salt on her skin. It was cooler here, the shade from the towering palms protecting them from the sweltering midday sun, but the water...it looked so inviting. *And* necessary.

Freddie was already stripping off his rash guard. 'Last one in's a rotten egg!'

'How old are...?' Her chastisement died on her lips as she lost herself in the ripple of his exposed abs, his pecs, his wide grin... She cleared her throat. 'Do I need to remind you we're not five any more?'

'And?'

She laughed.

'Are you sure it's safe in there? What if there's some river snake or...or...' She waved her hand about her helplessly, but his grin didn't waver.

'Philippe would have warned us. Come on, aren't you hot? Or are you chicken? A *very hot* chicken.'

She laughed more. 'I'm not chicken. Hot or otherwise!'

He lifted his brows at her, fisted his hands on his hips, drawing her eyes lower, and she gulped. 'I'm not... I'm just...cautious.'

'You look like you could do with a dip just as much as me.'

His eyes travelled over her, and her skin prickled beneath the layer of sweat that had her rash guard clinging ever more to her skin. But it wasn't the sun working its fiery magic, it was all Freddie and those eyes that seemed to tease and ignite in one.

'Don't worry, I've got you, Red.'

His voice and his words snagged at her heart and she bit into her lip.

'You nervous?'

'Why?'

'You're biting your lip.' He shrugged. 'It was always one of your things. That and chewing the corner of your mouth whenever you were nervous. Nervous or...'

He let the rest hang in the air unsaid and her heart bloomed along with the warmth building inside. Was there anything he didn't remember about her? And if he remembered so much, surely that meant something, that *she still meant* something, or at least she could still mean something if he let her.

And now she was thinking in riddles.

'I'm a little nervous.' Not of the water and what might lurk beneath the rocks any more, but of him and the way her heart was beating out of her control.

'Come on, Red, live a little.'

She was living a whole lot and that was the problem.

She nodded, not trusting her voice as she peeled her top over her head and tossed it to the ground beside his. Her hair clung to her neck and she shook it out before dipping to remove her shorts and adding them to the pile. Freddie hadn't moved an inch.

She sent him a look from beneath her lashes as she straightened and tiptoed to the water's edge, passing him by.

'Are you letting me win?' she said over her shoulder, and caught the way his heated gaze raked over her bikini-clad body, leaving her effectively stripped bare, her skin sensitised and eager for his touch.

'You'll forgive me if watching you strip distracted me somewhat.'

She shook her head, a smile teasing at her lips as she tried to brush off his compliment as a flippant remark, nothing more.

'Are you still a sore loser, Freddie?' She didn't wait for his response. Burying her worries for her heart, her sanity and what lay beneath the water, she jumped...and mentally cursed. It *was* cold.

But it was just what she needed, in more ways than one.

Breaking the surface, she let out a whoop, kicking her legs to tread water. She cleared her eyes, swept her hair back from her face and turned to see him still standing on the rocks.

'What was it you said—"I've got you, Red"?' she called out, grinning.

'Always.'

And with that he took a running leap, breaking the water a metre away and showering her as his promise hit home. *Always.* She kicked harder, told herself to quit it. But how could he say it and not really mean it?

And you shouldn't want—no, need—him to mean it!

'You did that on purpose!' she scolded when his head surfaced.

He turned to her, flicking his hair back off his forehead as he made for her.

'What?' His eyes danced, his closing proximity making her pulse race.

'Showering me with water!'

And making my heart swell with love for you.

She swallowed back the realisation.

Love.

Was she in love with him? Her face seemed to prickle with pins and needles, the warmth draining from it, and she forced a smile, needing to mask it as he got closer and closer.

No, it couldn't be. Not again. Not so soon. Falling, yes, not *fallen*.

He grinned. 'But you're already wet.'

She gulped at the naughty gleam in his eye, the double entendre very much intended, and she shoved water at him, backing away.

'And there I was thinking you're all grown up with your successful business, your charity...' She glared at him, trying to be playful and ignore the panicked beating of her heart. 'But really you're still a child.'

'I hope not.'

'You hope not?'

'Else I'd be worried about the nature of my thoughts right this second.'

She shook her head, her laugh heady in spite of the undercurrent within her. She swam back faster... The chase was always fun, wasn't it?

'You know you can't outswim me.'

'Wanna bet?'

Excitement bubbled up inside her and she let it, let herself feel like the teen she'd once been when he'd first looked at her like that.

'One delicious coconut!'

They quit their speedy strokes, their attention shifting to the rocks where Philippe now stood with said coconut held above his head. 'I'll leave it here for you and return in an hour or so. Would you like me to prepare it?'

'I reckon we can manage.'

She looked at Freddie in surprise and he shrugged. 'It can't be that hard surely?'

'Okay.'

Though she got the impression it had more to do with Freddie wanting them to be alone sooner than it did with his skill at preparing a coconut.

And she shouldn't be so dizzyingly excited by it.

She really shouldn't.

'*You* can crack a coconut?'

Jasmine waited until Philippe had left to ask the question and Freddie got the distinct impression it was a distraction technique. A way to question his ability while avoiding the heat fizzing between them and it made him grin all the more because he knew she felt it. He could see it in the way her eyes blazed, the way the colour crept into her cheeks, and he exulted that she was as powerless to stop it as he was.

He closed the distance between them. 'Yes.'

'Really?' Her eyes laughed at him, the water beading on her dark lashes making them all the more captivating as she backed away.

'Yes.' Another stroke forward. 'I've done it before.'

She nodded. 'Yeah, right, in between business meetings Stateside, you enjoy cracking open a coconut.'

'No, in fact, I—' He broke off as he realised what he'd been about to say.

'You?' She stilled, her brows nudging skywards, a smile dancing around her lips, and he wanted her smile to stay. That was why he didn't want to admit what he'd been about to.

'Nothing.'

'Come on, Freddie, just say it.'

He looked away, guilt weighing heavily in his gut. But he had no reason to feel guilty, they hadn't been together in for ever, and…well, time moved on.

Not so much your heart, though.

He ignored the inner gibe and clung to the sense that told him it was nothing for Jasmine to get upset over and in turn nothing for him to worry over either. And his heart had no place in this anyway.

'We sailed around the Caribbean for Dad's six-tieth, plenty of time for coconut hacking.'

'I see…' She frowned, the water rippling around her as she trod water. 'So why the hesitation?'

'I didn't want to dampen the moment by mentioning them.'

'Look, Freddie, they are your mum and dad, it's okay to talk about them. They only ever had your best interests at heart.'

He scoffed. 'I think it was more the case they had their own interests at heart.'

She shook her head. 'Seriously, Freddie, we were young back then, too young! Even you must see that now, with hindsight?'

Did he? Too young for marriage, perhaps. But surely it should have been their own decision to make, their own mistake to rectify.

'So, the Caribbean?' He knew she was trying to change the subject, clear the sudden cloud. 'Sounds lovely.'

'It was.'

Her frown returned. 'But?'

'But?'

'You don't look like it was lovely. In fact, you're acting kind of awkward still…'

'We were there with the Darlingtons.' His words came out with his breath, feeling very much like a confession.

Now she really frowned. 'The Darlingtons?'

'You know, Lord and Lady Darlington? Distant relations to the royal family, Darlingtons?'

'Oh, *those* Darlingtons. Don't they have a daughter about our...?' Her voice trailed off.

He saw the moment realisation hit, saw it in the way she looked away and the invisible cord that had been pulling them together in the water snapped.

'Is she the one your parents have in mind for you?'

He nodded, his jaw tense as he wished away this conversation entirely.

'Lady Sara Palmer-Darlington.' She nodded over her name. 'She's very beautiful. Isn't she the face of the designer Danielle? Not to mention her charity efforts and connections. Your parents must be beside themselves at the match.'

Her voice was strained and he wanted to reach for her, even though she was the one that had pushed them into this conversation.

He attempted a shrug. 'They can't seem to help themselves.'

'And you, can you help yourself, Freddie?' It blurted out of her and she bit her lip, the colour gone from her face, her eyes spiking with tears, and he cursed the whole situation, the way it made her feel, the way it made *him* feel. Guilty, and unreasonably so.

She turned and swam away and he followed, anger firing in his blood. 'There was a time when you told me I should listen to them, that they were right. Now you're, what? Telling me to fight back, to tell them that we live in an age where social status no longer matters when it comes to marriage and that I should be free to choose my own way?'

He sensed her flinch rather than saw it and knew he'd hit his mark.

'Shame you didn't feel that way ten years ago, Red.'

She stilled before the waterfall, her feet finding the rocky bottom at the edge of the lagoon, and she stepped forward, raising her head to the assault of the water.

And he hated it. He hated that she was shutting herself off from him. He hated that the past kept coming between them. He hated that he couldn't simply reach out and pull her into his arms, reassure her that she was the only woman he'd ever wanted to marry.

And why? Why tell her all that? She didn't deserve to hear those assurances from his lips. She was the one that had left, that had given up on them.

He stood behind her, his hands fisted at his sides.

'I was a child then.'

Her voice was a whisper disappearing in the rush of the water, but he heard it.

'You weren't a child. We were eighteen. We were—'

'We were too young for you to turn your back on your family.'

He shook his head, even though she couldn't see him. 'For all you say you left because they didn't approve, because *they* thought we were too young, it seems to me that you thought it too. It was *you* who left because deep down *you agreed.*'

She didn't even react and he pressed on, unable to stop.

'They would have come round eventually, Jas, they wouldn't have had a choice. I wouldn't have given them one.'

'And by then you would have been a changed man.'

'What do you mean?'

She spun into him, her head shaking as she gazed up at him imploringly. 'It doesn't matter. Just leave it, I shouldn't have— I didn't—'

'I want to know what you mean.' He was chilled to the bone and he wasn't letting this go. Not now.

Her eyes trembled as she stared at him, quiet, and then, 'You were already changing, don't you see? There were times when I'd catch you looking so anxious, so worried about us and the future, and the more your parents pushed back, the more determined you were. But…but…'

She waved a shaky hand up and down his chest,

her eyes lowering. 'It was tearing you apart, it was destroying you, taking away your happiness, the light in your eyes, the easy humour, the joy.'

'I was worried about the future, yes. I was worried about providing for us while still pursuing my degree if the worst happened and my family cut us off completely. I was worried you would be forced to give up your studies, your dreams. So, yes, Jas, I was worried, but—'

'Can't you see I didn't want that for you?' she interjected, her voice shaking with sincerity as tears joined the water already running down her face and he couldn't breathe for the pain of seeing hers. 'I'd see the worry in your face, and I'd try to tell myself it didn't matter, that as long as we loved one another we could get through it.'

'And we would have,' he blurted, his own hurt making his words harsh, 'if you'd only given us a chance.'

'But at what cost?'

She looked so fragile and pale before him now, her head tilted back, her hair dark with the water running through it.

'A cost I would have been willing to pay, Red.'

Her nose flared with her breath, her lashes fluttered. 'I wasn't.'

He stared at her, words failing him, movement too.

'Mum and me...' She took a deeper breath, her shoulders rolling back as she mustered her strength. 'There had always been just Mum and me, you know that. But you, you had a family, you were surrounded by love. I couldn't ask you to walk away from that and risk damaging you for ever.'

His smile was sad, cold with the truth of it. 'And yet I did it anyway.'

'You did, didn't you?' Her mouth quivered, her arms wrapping around her middle. 'I was shocked when Mum told me you'd left Oxford and got yourself into Harvard.'

'I was angry.'

'But Oxford was your dream.'

'No, *you* were my dream.'

Her eyes widened, glistening anew. 'I'm sorry, Freddie. I just couldn't take the risk. I couldn't take the risk that one day you would turn around and regret it. And Mum…well, you were always so feisty and quick to act, she worried that your parents backing you into a corner gave you all the more reason to stand your ground—'

He went to object, his anger building with her honesty, but she wasn't stopping. It was rushing out of her, her eyes ablaze with it.

'—to stand and fight, and that—that it might not have been about love at all, and that one day when life settled down again and the fight was over you'd regret it and then where would you be? It would be awful and devastating and… I don't know…'

Finally, she trailed off, her hands gripping her upper arms, her eyes not leaving his.

'You should have known me better than that.' His voice was raw with the pain of it, the anger, the disbelief.

'But I did know you, Freddie, I knew how loyal and loving you were, and those traits tied you to me just as much as they tied you to your family.'

Her words were chipping away at the age-old hurt, shining a new light on an old understanding. His family life versus hers. It hadn't just been about social standing, a divide they couldn't overcome, it had been about the bonds of love, of family, of her worry for him.

'I couldn't bear it, your parents' disapproval, my mother's concern,' she stressed into the quiet. 'I couldn't bear you giving up everything for me. I loved you too much to risk your regret, to have you blame me with time, hate me even.'

'I could *never* have hated you.'

'That's not quite true.'

'It is.'

'You hated me when I left.'

Her eyes blazed up at him, her sincerity wrapping around his heart, teasing at the mess of emotion inside.

'I wanted to hate you, Jas.' He took a shaky breath. 'It would have been so much easier if I could have hated you.'

They fell quiet, the rush of the water, the wildlife falling away too as they both absorbed the power of his confession, the meaning of it.

'I—I tried to find you after you left Oxford,' she said softly. 'I was worried, but you were nowhere to be found.'

His brows drew together, surprise making his question choke out of him. 'You did?'

'Yes. I left to protect you from making that decision, and then you went and did it anyway and I wanted to find you, I wanted… I knew you wouldn't want to see me, but…'

'I travelled. I took some time out to reimagine my future after you took ours away. I couldn't stand being in Scotland, I couldn't stand being in the UK. I wanted to get as far away as I could.'

'Far away from me.'

He swallowed, ignored the clawing sensation in his gut. 'Not just you, my family too. At first I blamed you for not having faith in me, for taking that choice away. Then I blamed them for making you feel it wasn't a choice in the first place.'

'And now? Now that you've achieved all you have without me—?'

'Now that you've achieved all you have without me, you mean.'

She took a breath, gave a small nod, her words quiet. 'If I'm completely honest, I'm not sure our relationship could have survived trying to pursue our careers, coping with our families' disapproval and all the growing up we had left to do.

I don't want to hurt you, and I'm still sorry that I left, but—but can you honestly say you think we would have stayed together had I not left?'

He couldn't speak. His gut ached, his heart too. And not because he thought she was wrong…

He reached out, his palm soft on her cheek as her words sank in, struck a chord with such resonance he felt choked by it.

She covered his hand against her cheek and he closed his eyes to shut out the pain he could see in hers. She was right. So very right.

He opened his eyes slowly, took in all that was exquisite in her glistening green gaze.

'As much as it pains me to admit it…' he cupped her other cheek, held her in his hands '…you're right. Not in the way that you left… I can't…' He swallowed, fending off the painful memory. 'But then I didn't give you a choice. I was going into that room declaring my love for you, come hell or high water.'

'I know.' Her lashes fluttered over fresh tears as her lips quivered into the smallest of smiles. 'And I loved you for it. I may not have had the same confidence, but it didn't mean I didn't love you.'

Her declaration warmed his heart, soothed the pain.

'But now what, Freddie? What do we do now?'

'Now…'

He thought about it and felt his gut roll, his skin

prickle. They were at an impasse. Their lives had had no space for them ten years ago; they had even less room for them now.

But they had this. Their week. This was a known entity. No one could get hurt because there was no commitment, no expectation.

Not like there had been all those years ago.

'Now we're here in paradise, no outside world looking in, and I want to make the most of it.'

She blinked up at him, a battle still raging in her eyes, but he was ready to forget again. Forget and live for now.

He bowed his head, but she pressed her palm into his chest.

'Don't you think it's time, though, Freddie?'

'Time?' He frowned.

'Yes, time to fight back.'

'Fight back?' He straightened, his frown deepening.

'Yes.' She wet her lips. 'To put your foot down once and for all with your parents and tell them you have no interest in a marriage of their choosing. Not now, not ever.'

His mouth lifted to one side. 'I've never stopped fighting back, Jas. I fought for you ten years ago and walked out. I've lived in America ever since.'

'That's not fighting, Freddie, that's avoidance, just as this trip with M has been.'

He thought about it. About the conversations

with his parents over the years, his desire to keep the peace but also his distance. All to avoid conflict.

'And you won't have the ocean between you soon. You'll be home and you'll have to face it…unless…' she eyed him, her fingers flexing against his chest '… Lady Sara *is* what you want?'

A laugh-cum-scoff erupted. He couldn't help it. There was only one woman he could ever envisage at the head of the aisle, and admitting it out loud wasn't happening. Instead, he told a different truth…more avoidance…but he couldn't risk exposing the truth in his heart.

'Sara's a good woman, intelligent, kind, but Jas, it would be like marrying my mother. And, believe me, Sara knows how I feel, I've never strung her along.'

'It's a shame your parents can't get the same message.'

'They will do,' he said, putting all the determination he felt into his voice as he lowered his hands to her hips and pulled her closer. 'I promise.'

'No more running?'

'No more running.'

'Good.'

'Now can we stop talking about my parents?'

'Why?'

'Because talk of them is ruining all my plans

for this waterfall and you and everything I want to do…'

He pressed her body up against his own and kissed her, caught her sweet little sigh with his groan.

'I like the sound of that,' she murmured against his lips, her hands hooking around his neck, her slight frame fitting so perfectly against him and soothing away the painful remnants of old. As for the future…

He deepened the kiss, lifting her as she wrapped her legs around him, and he spun them back under the waterfall, let the pummelling flow pound the back of his head, his neck, his shoulders, anything to beat back the panicked pounding of his heart. The alarm bells ringing so very loud now.

But he wouldn't listen. He couldn't.

He wanted her, for as long as this week would allow, and the pieces of his shattered heart would just have to fall where they may.

He'd survived before. He could survive her again.

CHAPTER TEN

JASMINE LOOKED AT the various outfits strewn across the bed. What did one wear to a couples cooking class when it wasn't all about the cooking but the romance of it?

And, yes, she was trying to tell herself this was heading nowhere, that in four days they would be going their separate ways, but that voice was getting quieter and quieter. Because facing up to their past, talking about it and her reasons for leaving, she felt the glimmer of hope swell.

She wasn't the wallflower she'd once been. The one so fearful of the future, of tearing apart his family, she couldn't see past the bad to keep hold of the good—him.

She lifted the navy palazzo pants she'd pulled out earlier, the linen fabric perfect for the early evening warmth, the colour forgiving enough should she make an absolute mess while trying to impress Freddie with her non-existent cookery skills. She picked up the navy camisole also on the bed and held them together, turning to face the mirror that filled one wall. Practical and subtly sexy. Perfect.

She eyed her hair, beachy waves kinking up her strands even though she'd showered since their kayaking. If she was honest, she liked it. It softened her cheekbones and jawline, made her cheeks look rosy and fuller, and her eyes bigger, greener.

And it's just the sun and sea doing all that, not the man who's put the spring back in your step.

Her lips flickered into a smile, her mind replaying their conversation at the waterfall. He'd said he couldn't hate her, and his eyes had very definitely shone. It had to be more than just desire, pure sex, surely?

The vibration of her phone from beneath the pile of clothes brought an end to her confusing thoughts and she tossed her outfit onto the bed to dig it out.

It was M.

Or, more specifically, Madison Morgan, the owner of M.

In all the excitement, she'd forgotten this call would be coming. The call to check in on their 'date' and she certainly hadn't prepared herself for it. She considered letting it ring out because, seriously, what could she say other than the truth.

But it hardly felt fair to avoid a conversation with the woman whose team had worked so hard to match her and Freddie together in the first place.

Maybe Madison had already spoken to Freddie, in which case she already knew that they had history and Jasmine wouldn't need to be the one to break the news. But what was to say Freddie would admit to it? Not that he was a liar, but it was hardly straightforward.

She forced a smile, even though Madison couldn't see her. 'Hello?'

'Jasmine, hi! I'm so glad I've caught you!'

'Hey, Madison, you've actually just caught me between activities.' Her cheeks bloomed with colour. Why did 'activities' sound so much like a euphemism?

For the same reason your body overheats at the mere mention of Freddie!

'Ah, fabulous, what is it you have this evening? In fact, I have it all here…ah, cookery!'

'Yes.' She toyed with the hem of the slip she was wearing, her mind wandering ahead to cooking up close with Freddie. 'Couples cooking the creole way.'

'From what I know, it's a lot of seafood, curry and fruit.'

She laughed. 'That sounds about right.'

'And are you liking the Seychelles?'

'I love it here.' Which was the honest truth, but Jasmine had a feeling she'd love being anywhere as long as her match remained the same. 'It truly is paradise.'

'Ah, I'm so glad. You actually have your match to thank for the location.'

'I do?' She frowned, surprise making her voice soft.

'Yes. Usually when I ask the question, with men

especially, what location they think of when I say the word "romance", they often give a vague response, or think about it for a bit. But Freddie came straight out with it so we knew that just had to be the location. And it certainly fitted your requirement for somewhere hot, did it not?'

She couldn't find her voice as the hope she was trying to keep contained completely ran away with her.

'Jasmine, are you still there?'

'Yes. Yes. Sorry, I was distracted.' Distracted by the fact that Freddie had chosen the Seychelles. Distracted by the fact that romance plus holiday still meant the Seychelles for him. Did that in itself mean more? That the Freddie who had loved her wasn't too far beneath the surface, despite the passage of time and their history?

And yet he could have been here with someone else entirely if M hadn't chosen her.

A timely reminder to put hope back where it belonged. Shut tight in a sealed box.

'And was he right?'

She could hear the hope in Madison's voice too, could picture her brown eyes all soft and warm, just like they'd been in her initial interview when she'd asked Jasmine what she was looking for in her perfect man.

And what had she been looking for? Freddie, all Freddie. He'd been her perfect man ten years ago, and he was still as perfect now, even more so with a maturity, a measured control that could only come with age and experience.

'Ooh, I wish I'd video-called, all this silence is hard to cope with.'

Jasmine gave a small laugh. 'Sorry, no, it's… it's perfect.'

'As *romantic* as Freddie hoped?'

Was it? From what Freddie had told her, he hadn't been hoping for romance at all when he'd embarked on this little adventure—another reason to keep hope packed away.

But without hope she felt bereft, and she wouldn't ruin the last few days walking around with fear hot on her tail.

'It *is* romantic.' She thrust positivity into her voice and tried to feel it too. 'Very romantic!'

'That's wonderful, I'm sure Freddie will agree, then.'

'You've not spoken to him yet?'

'No, I did try him first but there was no answer.'

'I imagine he's in the shower, getting ready.'

Or had he ignored the call? Was he, like she had been, worried about what to say?

'Is that right?' There was a smile—or was it a smug smirk?—in Madison's voice. 'Always a positive sign when the client knows what their date is up to.'

Jasmine's laugh was more of a scoff as nerves got the better of her. 'We've not long been back from kayaking and I've been getting ready myself.'

'Well, it's good that I've caught you on your own. I do like to talk to my clients individually if possible. You wouldn't believe how hard that can be sometimes.' Madison gave a soft laugh and Jasmine could just imagine why it was so hard, or was that her insatiable appetite for Freddie getting in the way again?

'So-o-o,' Madison cooed, 'how's it going?'

Jasmine bit her lip. How *was* it going? 'It's... it's interesting.'

'Good interesting, bad interesting?'

'Good, definitely good.' Or at least she hoped it was.

'Are you going to expand on "interesting"?'

Jasmine laughed at Madison's eager persistence. She liked the woman a lot. She was easy to talk to and had the amazing ability to coax things out of her that Jasmine hadn't even been aware of thinking or feeling before. Rather like Sadie and Izzy, she was like the best friend you always wanted, or the big sister you wish you had. It felt like she had your back and cared passionately, when in reality she was a very expensive and very successful matchmaker.

Though there was no reason she couldn't be all of the above...

'Am I only getting a laugh?'

'It's complicated,' she said, flustered.

'Ooh, three days in and it's already complicated. Should I start planning the wedding out-fit now?'

As if. Jasmine's laugh was well and truly high, her mind as delirious as her body as she pictured it. Freddie at the head of the aisle, her walking down it…and the severe and disapproving High-groves, if they even attended at all. And there the scene shattered into a million pieces.

'So, it's a good kind of interesting *and* compli-cated. You know, I say this about all my clients, but you two in particular gave me such a good feeling, a definite match made in heaven.'

Jasmine plopped down onto the bed, her sigh wistful and wishful in one. She caught sight of herself in the mirror, the silly little smile that played about her lips, her eyes that glistened. 'I wish.'

And she'd really just said that out loud…

'Why does that sound like a hopeless "I wish"?' Madison asked, her frown evident in her voice.

'Like I said, it's complicated.' She took a breath and let it out swiftly. 'Freddie and I have history.'

'What?'

'Yes, we know each other. In fact, we grew up together. My mother was the housekeeper of his family home.'

'You're kidding!' Jasmine had to hold the phone away from her ear. 'But neither of you mentioned one another in your dating history, unless of course you never…'

'Well, I think that's because we both tried—' *and failed* '—to forget.'

Maybe the odds would be more in their favour now if they hadn't had that history to share. What would it be like, meeting Freddie afresh?

Silly question. She'd have fallen just as swiftly, especially without the first-hand knowledge of his family to put her off.

'To forget? So…it didn't work out…well, of course it didn't work out or else you wouldn't be here now, but…you know…goodness, this is a bit awkward. You just couldn't write this.'

Madison's flurry of words had Jasmine feeling a strange sense of guilt. They'd truly landed her in a pickle, not intentionally, but still, she felt bad and she wanted to reassure her that it wasn't M's system messing up. No, that was all down to her and Freddie.

'Don't worry, it's not your fault and if I'm honest, your system did call it right. Freddie is as much my ideal man now as he was back then.'

'But—but you parted ways?'

'When we were eighteen, I actually… I called off our engagement.'

'No way!'

'Yes way. We were young, it was too much too soon, and it was tricky, with his parents and me being the housekeeper's daughter—it was hardly an ideal match in their eyes, not when they had their sights set on a high society bride.'

'I see.'

'And my mother wasn't best pleased, as you can imagine. They were her employers at the end of the day.'

'And her employers didn't think her daughter was good enough. Oh, no!'

'Precisely.'

'But, oh, my!' Madison exclaimed. 'You were star-crossed lovers! You were meant to be, but were separated by opposing forces. That's so incredibly romantic, tragic but romantic.'

Jasmine laughed with a frown. 'I guess you could put it like that.'

'And here we are now—' she could hear the budding excitement in Madison's voice '—with a chance for you to rewrite your paths, make it work and put all that behind you.'

'I'd like to think so.'

Maybe it was the loss of her mum, the realisation that life was too short, the realisation that what she felt for him had stood the test of time... she didn't know. But those reasons for ending it when she had been eighteen held no weight now and had no bearing on their future either. Yes, changes would need to be made, the kind of changes she hadn't been willing to make for Tim, but for Freddie, for the two of them...

But what was to say Freddie would feel the same? Even if he could trust her with his heart again, would he want to make space in his life for her?

'You're still worried about how his parents will receive you?'

'No. Not really.' And she wasn't. She wasn't the insecure teen she'd once been and she believed that, whatever happened, Freddie had already broken away and found a way to maintain his ties to them. A relationship with her would do no more damage than had already been done, but... 'I'm not even sure Freddie will give us another chance to get to that hurdle.'

'How so?'

'He seems determined to go it alone.'

'What? Life? That's not the impression he gave us.'

Oh, dear, she'd put her foot in it. 'I mean, I don't think he knows how to share his life with someone else.'

She wasn't sure that sounded any better either, but she was trying to be honest.

'Then you just have to show him how good it can be.'

'Oh, I'm trying.'

'Have you been honest with him, told him that you want to try and make a go of it?'

'Not outright. We've dealt with the past, though, and that's something. As for the future...'

Freddie seemed so focused on keeping this

week as just that—a week. But she wanted more, so much more.

'Well, there you go, you just need to be honest with him and good things will happen!'

She wished she could share Madison's confidence.

'We've brought you together for a reason, Jasmine, a very good reason, I'm sure of it.'

'I hope you're right.'

'I'm always right when it comes to love.'

She gave a shaky laugh and heard Madison let go of another dreamy sigh. 'I can't believe it. In all the days of M this is most definitely a first.'

'It does feel rather unbelievable.'

'Like a wish coming true.'

'Yes.' Jasmine had certainly wished for a fairy godmother to wave a magic wand back then, and now she had Freddie back in her life again she wished above all else to keep him there.

'Second chance romances have always been a favourite of mine.'

Jasmine smiled. 'Mine too.'

'Well, I'd best let you get on with living your real-life fairy tale with Freddie. This has made my year and it's only July.'

Jasmine grinned, buoyed up by Madison's optimism. 'We're not quite hitched yet, you know.'

'Ah, give it time and I'll be adding a second chance romance to my repertoire. It doesn't get any better than that...'

Jasmine was still smiling as she hung up the phone and busied herself getting ready.

Madison was right, there was only one way to find out if this was going to work and that was to be honest with Freddie, to lay her cards on the table and hope for the best.

Sooner rather than later.

CHAPTER ELEVEN

COOKING WITH JASMINE was an experience.

Her ability to burn something no sooner than she looked at it was quite special. But it was her continuous laughter and those dancing green eyes that were getting to him.

She'd been late arriving at the outdoor cooking pavilion because Madison had caught up with her. A call he'd not been as confident as her to take. He didn't want to pick apart how he felt or lay out their history to an outsider, and he certainly didn't want to lie.

Madison Morgan had a good heart, her business was quite clearly her passion, so it was bad enough that he'd strung the agency along to keep his parents at bay, but to speak to her now when he was struggling to keep a handle on how he felt...

'Don't you like it?' Jasmine frowned at him from across the candlelit table, calling his attention to the fact that he'd barely touched the dish they'd cooked together, and the way she was looking at him suggested she'd been watching him for far too long.

'Sorry, I zoned out.'

'A penny for them?'

His laugh was tight as he shook his head. 'You don't want to know.'

'You'd be surprised.'

He smiled at her and dropped his eyes to the dish, loaded up his fork. 'I think it's nice. What about you?'

He gestured to her plate, aware that they were very much alone again, and she'd chosen to time her question with their first dose of privacy since the cookery lesson had begun. It felt like the opening to something much deeper than talk over the food and he wasn't ready for it.

'Yes, it's tasty. I have to admit I'm glad we made the grilled fish and *satini*. I really didn't fancy the flying bat dish.'

His laugh was much easier now. '*Les Roussettes* certainly gives it a better ring.'

'Until you realise what it means! And I'm surprised you didn't know. You aced languages at school.'

'In my defence, it's not often you discuss fruit bats in class.'

'True.' She grinned, her eyes turning skywards just as the said *roussettes* swept overhead. 'Although now I feel bad, insulting them when they're flying above us right now.'

'Er... I think they'd actually be *relieved* we don't want to eat them.'

She smiled, but steadily the humour dissipated in her expression, her brows easing together, the curve to her lips turning down.

Definitely a conversation brewing, and definitely not one that he wanted. They'd done enough talking at the waterfall.

He threw his focus into eating, though tasting was proving impossible with the uneasy churn in his gut. By the time they'd devoured dessert, he was more than ready to cut off the discussion with more of what he knew how to give and enjoy— pleasure.

He stood and held out his hand. 'Shall we?'

She blinked up at him, those big green eyes working a magic that went far deeper than he was willing to allow.

She slipped her hand inside his. 'I was hoping we could take a walk...on the beach?'

'Walking wasn't quite what I had in mind.'

She laughed, the sound joyous after the strained quiet, her playful nudge in his side with her elbow all the more so. 'Freddie!'

'What? I'm here on a beautiful island, with a beautiful woman. I think it's completely under-standable that I might want to do something other than walk.'

'Well, tough. We're walking.'

*And talking...*he reluctantly acknowledged. Though it was silence that accompanied their stroll along the subtly lit trail down to the beach. Glass-dome-covered candles were being used to ensure the sense of romance was never far away. M truly had chosen well with this resort.

And M was the reason he knew this conversation was brewing now.

The sounds of nocturnal wildlife filled the silence, the incessant chatter taking the edge off the silence stretching between them.

'And they say New York is the city that never sleeps…' He was making conversation—*safe* conversation. 'This place seems to have a constant on switch too.'

She smiled up at the stars as she released his hand and hooked her arm through his, drawing him closer. 'I like it, though; it's comforting to know you're not the only one awake when you can't sleep.'

'Do you often find yourself feeling that way?' There was just something in the way she'd said it…

'What way?'

'Awake and…' He shrugged. 'Feeling alone?'

There was that word again: alone. But it beat lonely…even though he knew he meant it in the same way. The same way she'd meant it when she'd said it to him that first night at dinner…

'Sometimes. Nature certainly beats the sounds of the city, and though you get the odd cat cry or shrill fox call, this is definitely more soothing.'

He nodded as he tried to ignore the way his chest ached. The idea of her lying awake in an empty bed, feeling that way. The idea that he could be beside her too swift to follow. No. Just no.

But the image nagged at him anyway. As did the uneasy realisation that he'd let her believe countless women had shared his bed over the years, when the truth was very different.

'You know when I told you...' He cleared his throat '...when I implied that I rarely slept alone, it wasn't quite true...'

'No?'

She looked up at him and he could sense the smile on her lips, not that he dared look as he explained, 'The truth is I hardly have time for even that. More often than not it's more trouble than it's worth.'

'It's only trouble if it's the wrong person.'

He risked a glimpse, saw so much shining back in her gaze and looked away just as swiftly.

'Perhaps.' *She's right and you know she's right*, came the nagging inner voice.

'It seems to me we both need to get a better work-life balance. We should find a way to make time for—for finding the right person.'

He didn't miss her hesitation and he knew what she wasn't saying. That they'd found the right person, they just needed to find the time to carve out a future together.

'I thought you had as much interest in finding love as I did?'

He tried to inject a joviality to his tone, make it into a tease, but it fell flat.

'I've had time to think since then, to reconsider what it is I want from life, and talking to Madison kind of helped put it into perspective for me.'

He tried not to tense up, but he knew his arm locked in hers as his step faltered just a little.

'Did you— Did she manage to get hold of you? She said she tried to reach you before she called me, but there was no answer.'

He swallowed, kept his eyes fixed on the waves crashing in the distance rather than on her up-turned face. The sea was rougher tonight and it matched his mood. The tumultuous chaos of what this was, what it could be, and the fact he wanted to run and stay in one.

'No. She rang, but…'

He let his silence do the rest, and she lowered her gaze, leaned her head into him. 'I know. It's a difficult conversation to navigate.'

'Did you tell her everything?'

She snuck a look up at him and still he couldn't look at her. 'Yes. Well, I had to, really. I was always a rubbish liar and let's face it, M outdid themselves matching us together.'

'That's true.'

'I only gave her the high-level details, enough for her to understand what went wrong. She called us…'

Her voice trailed off and he frowned down at her. 'She called us what?'

Her smile was small, a hint of colour in her

cheeks just visible in the moonlight. 'Star-crossed lovers.'

His chuckle was tight. 'Quite the contemporary Romeo and Juliet.'

'Well, not entirely as our families weren't sworn enemies.'

'No...'

'It came down to social standing.'

'It was as much an issue for your mother as it was mine.' He didn't know why he felt the need to even out the blame, but he did. And still he felt guilty as she nodded her acceptance of it.

'Ultimately, I guess it was.'

They reached the end of the path, the white sand stretched out before them, the moonlight reflecting off the water as the waves continued to crash into the night.

'I meant what I said, Jas. No more avoiding. I will set my parents straight. I know I'm hurting our relationship more by not dealing with it.'

She turned to give him a small smile, and he hooked his hands around her waist, looked into her eyes.

'The thing is, deep down I know they'll stand by me. That they might be annoyed, disappointed even, but ultimately I'm still their son...'

'They'll still love you,' she said softly.

'Yes.'

Her brow creased, her eyes lowering to his chest. 'It makes me wonder...'

'Wonder what?'

She met his gaze, quiet for a beat. 'Whether we could make it work now… Whether we could try and—'

'Don't, Jas…' The tension coiled back through him exponentially. 'Let's not ruin what we have now with talk of an impossible future.'

'Why is it impossible? You've already said you're going to make a stand against your parents so there's no reason we can't take control of our own destinies, write our own future. Together.'

'Is that what Madison said to you?'

She shrugged softly. 'She may have said something like that, but these are my thoughts, my words. We are stronger now, wiser. We can make this work if we both want it enough.'

'Why is now any different to how it was back then? My family are still the same, the circles they move in, that I will move in…'

'But we're not the same.'

He shook his head, looked to the heavens as though they would throw him an answer that would end this torture. Because it *was* torture to be handed everything he had ever wanted and not be able to take it.

'We have less time now than we ever had. You and Tim broke up because your work came first. I've been there too. We don't have time for ourselves, let alone others.'

'We can make time.'

'It's not that simple, and you know it. I have the charity, I have the company and I have a future back in Scotland—an estate, a title, responsibilities that I have to take on.'

'Together we can—'

'Jas, stop it. *Please.*'

'Why? What is it you're so afraid of?'

'History repeating itself! Don't you see, Jas, we do this, we commit and it falls apart...' He couldn't even breathe for the pain of it, and he gripped her shoulders, dropped his forehead to hers as he sought the strength he needed. 'You wouldn't risk me hating you ten years ago, and I won't risk you hating me now.'

'I could nev—'

He pressed his thumb to her lips, stared down into her eyes. 'Please, Jas. Don't throw my words back at me.'

She went very still and he wanted to take it all back, the hurt he knew he was inflicting, but he couldn't. He wouldn't give her the hope he'd once foolishly possessed, but he would take the strength she'd once possessed to walk away.

He eased his thumb from her lips, cupped her face in his hands. 'We agreed a week, no harm, no foul...no pain.'

'But don't you at least want to try?' She raised her hands to his hair, her fingers gently caressing. 'Don't you want to take the opportunity M has given us to take a chance on us now? Madison reckons—'

'Madison reckons!' He started, anger sparking that she would ask him to take a chance on them when she hadn't been willing to all those years ago. It didn't matter that the anger was irrational, unfair even, sparked by panic, fear—he just needed this conversation over. The dizzying mess with hope at its heart. Hope that Madison, that Jasmine were right. The kind of hope that had the power to crush him all over again. 'Madison is a romantic, an idealist, and it's in her interest to see us work out. I would take what she says with a pinch of salt.'

Her fingers stilled in his hair. 'That's a bit harsh.'

'Harsh was what you were back then!'

Her sudden pallor gutted him, her paleness so much worse for the light of the moon as her hands fell away.

'I'm sorry— I didn't— I don't…'

There were no words in the face of her pain and he hated himself for hurting her, but he hated their past and the confusion more.

The heavy night air surrounded them, the insects and the waves punctuating the strained silence, but there was nothing he could say, nothing he could do.

She pulled away from him, slipped off her sandals and walked down to where the waves were rolling in.

'Your trousers will get wet. Be careful!'

She didn't seem to hear him, just carried on going until she was walking in the shallows, her whole demeanour defeated, broken, and it was killing him.

She looked so beautiful—beautiful and broken.

He'd never wanted to hold her in his arms more and felt her so off limits.

He walked towards her. 'Red?'

She paused and turned to him, her eyes dark and glittering.

'We have this time now,' he tried softly, 'let's not take it away with the past.'

Her smile lifted to one side. 'You're the one letting the past intervene.'

'No, I'm keeping it real. I'm giving the past the nod it deserves and the future... I'm protecting us both, just as you did back then.'

She looked out over the ocean. 'You and I have a different version of what the past deserves, Freddie.'

He closed the distance between them, desperate to reconnect, to feel the calm only she could provide. And he knew how messed up that was.

'Let us have the now, please, I beg of you.' He reached out to touch her chin, gently encouraging her to look at him. 'Please understand, I can't go through that pain again, Red, I can't.'

Who are you really trying to convince? Yourself or her?

'But I promise you this right now, I want you and nobody else. Just you. For the time we're here, I will treasure you, I will care for you, I will worship the ground you walk on.'

'And afterwards?' she whispered.

He felt his heart shatter and reformed it with ice. 'Afterwards we go our separate ways, just like before.'

'But…but you'll be in Edinburgh. *I'll* be in Edinburgh.'

'It's a big city, nothing to say we need see each other again.'

He would never be as weak as he'd once been. He couldn't. As for the future, there was no avoiding it. He would be the Laird of Highgrove, and with all the responsibility, the demands on his time, he wouldn't treat her to the scraps that were left over when work was done, and the estate was tended to. He wouldn't be his father.

She shuddered before him and he wrapped his arms around her.

'You're cold.' Though he sensed it wasn't the coolness of the sea or the late hour that had made her so. 'We should head back.'

They retraced their steps, his arm around her, holding her close, but he felt as distant from her as he had been these last ten years.

When they reached the fork in the path, the one that led to his quarters or hers, she turned to look at him and he tugged her towards him, tugged her and struggled to keep his heart in its icy grip.

It's okay to want her now and let her go later...

He only wished he felt the assurance all the way through his once bitten heart that seemed determined to warm, to care, to dream.

'I should probably stay in my room tonight.' She tried to pull away.

'No.' It was out before he could stop it, his arms coming around her as he forced himself to ask, 'Unless that's what you really want?'

'No, Freddie.' She shook her head, her eyes awash with tears, and a lump formed in his throat, making it difficult to breathe, to swallow. 'I want to stay with you.'

'Then come with me,' he managed to say.

'How can you ask that after all you said?'

'Because I never said I wanted this to end now. I want this time with you, Jas. I want this time to forget all else but you.'

He could see the fight in her, could see it and feared it, and so he kissed her. It was a dirty trick. It was cruel to use their mutual desire to keep her. But it was crueller still to torture themselves by separating sooner than their time on the island allowed.

She froze for a split second, her mouth unmoving under his, and then she was kissing him back, her entire body melting into him.

'Please, Red...' He brushed the words against her lips.

She nodded, a murmured acceptance, and he pulled her into his side, kissed the top of her head as relief coursed through him.

They headed towards his room in step together.

'So, since you know the M itinerary off by heart, what do they have in store for us tomorrow?' Her question was soft, quiet, and he knew she was seeking a light distraction from the heavy echo of their fallout.

'Sailing... We're taking a trip out to Praslin Island.'

'Oh, sailing. That should be fun.'

Fun.

Exactly what this week should be about, and he needed to get better at keeping her focused on that.

She sank deeper into him and he relished it, her willingness to give herself over to the force still pulling them together.

He only wished the force was more powerful than that which had torn them apart. But the pain, the belief that she would run from the force that was his family, his heritage was still there, stronger than ever.

Because above all, he was a Highgrove, and he couldn't ever shake that off.

CHAPTER TWELVE

SAILING WAS NOT FUN!

In fact, Jasmine would go as far as to say it was the very opposite of fun and actually torture.

And she had no idea what she'd done to deserve it, but if she didn't get back on land soon, she feared breakfast would be making a reappearance, not to mention their lovingly prepared dishes the night before.

And thinking about that really wasn't helping…

'Hey.' Freddie's voice was soft in her ear, but not soft enough for her over-sensitised body and she flinched away, even more when his hand touched her back. 'Sorry.'

She sensed him ease back but couldn't risk a peek, she was too busy trying to breathe steadily and slowly, just like they had been advised, but it wasn't working. The catamaran lurched as the waves buffeted it again and she gripped the handrail tightly.

'I don't remember you ever being seasick.'

'I don't ever remember being on a boat that rocked like it was about to capsize before.'

Ooh, too many words. And breathe.

She heard Freddie laugh. The low sound was no longer sexy. Not in the slightest. If she was capable of it, she'd show him just what she thought of his laugh, but that last stream of words had cost her dearly.

'It's hardly going to capsize, Red. It's a gentle rocking motion at worst. Like the kind you'd use to send a baby off to sleep.'

'Less of the rocking,' she said through gritted teeth.

'Try tricking your body into believing you're on land, and that everything is a figment of your imagination.'

She moaned into her fist.

'You only *feel* sick because your inner ear is sending different signals from those that your eyes are sending.'

'Signals?' she blurted. She really couldn't care less about signals, and what they were or weren't doing.

'That's right, different signals than those your eyes are sending. It causes your body to get confused, so try telling it something different.'

'Something different.' She could hardly believe what he was suggesting, let alone do it.

Like it's that simple.

He merely smiled, his blue eyes vibrant and... *Hang on.*

'Are you laughing at me?'

'No.' His face fell, his body straightening.

'You are!' His eyes were definitely dancing...or was it just the effect of the waves being reflected back—? *Oh, no, the waves!*

She buried her head back in her arms.

'I'm trying to distract you.'

'It's not helping, Freddie.'

'It's a shame, it really is beautiful out here.'

Oh, she knew it was beautiful all right, she'd seen enough of it. Before the nausea, stomach cramps and vom— No, she hadn't vomited, not yet, but she wasn't sure how far off that was. And she really didn't want to vomit.

'Ooh, there's a turtle.'

'What?' Her head shot up, her eyes eagerly scanning the clear water.

'*See*. Distracting you.'

'Freddie!' She punched him in the chest, reassuming her position as her stomach cramped. She was going to kick him if he carried on being this helpful.

'Maybe a little sip of water.'

She groaned.

'A ginger ale?'

'No.' She pursed her lips, not that he could see now her head was once more buried in her arms. She must look positively grey, or was it green?

Whoa! The boat lurched again, sending her rocking back and her head up.

'How long?' she blurted.

'How long, what?'

She made a noise with her mouth. Surely it was obvious. 'How long until we get to land?'

'An hour maybe.'

And then they'd have to board the boat again to get back…

She groaned audibly and he must have sensed the direction of her thoughts as he said, 'The captain reckons it won't be quite as bad this afternoon for the return leg to Rosalie.'

Phew. At least that was something, and she murmured her gratitude to the floor.

'You want to hear something sweet?'

He didn't wait for her to reply, which was good because she wasn't planning on saying another word.

'Rosalie Island got its name from a French naval officer. He explored it back in the late seventeen-hundreds and named it after his wife. Quite a gift. Not that he ever came back to see it, or his wife for that matter…'

'He didn't see his wife again. Or she didn't get to see the island?'

'She didn't get to see it.'

'Oh.'

Freddie carried on, his smooth chatter flowing over her, and she found it became less of an annoyance and more of a lulling murmur, his little titbits of information giving her something to focus on other than the rolling of her stomach. He didn't touch her again, he'd learned his lesson there, but he stayed beside her, his attention very much on her when he should have been enjoying the view.

* * *

Over an hour later, her toes curling into soft, warm sand, she managed a meek smile. Land at last. 'Thank you.'

He grinned at her, his sunglasses hiding his eyes. 'For being annoying?'

'I'm sorry. You weren't annoying, I just…' She grimaced, her hand gripping her stomach. 'I've never been seasick before. I didn't know it was a thing for me, or how awful it could be.'

'It's fine, it's not your fault.' He frowned at her hand gesture and looked to where their guide for the day was waiting patiently in the shade of a thatched shack and chatting with new arrivals from another boat. 'Are you sure you're up for this trek?'

She followed his line of sight, felt the heat of the day beating down on her beneath her cap and the truth was she didn't feel it. She felt like she was still on the boat, rocking with the sea, and gritted her teeth as she swallowed down the sudden moisture in her mouth.

'Tell you what,' he said, 'why don't I see if we can rest here for a bit?'

She frowned at him. 'I don't want to waste their time.'

'It's okay, I'm sure they won't mind.'

'But they might be busy later.'

'And if they *are* busy…' he pushed his sunglasses back and the compassion in his vibrant blue eyes made her belly flutter rather than roll '…we'll make the most of Praslin's shoreline. It's beautiful here.'

'It's as beautiful as Rosalie and we're staying there,' she murmured, unconvinced. She didn't want to spoil this for him too. 'When will you get chance to see the wildlife here again and the Vallée de Mai Nature Reserve?'

He cupped her cheek, the move so soft and surprising it stole her breath. 'Stop fretting and sit down before you fall down.'

'Am I swaying?'

His smile lifted to one side. 'Just a little. And if the sea doesn't improve, I'll see if I can get us a flight back to Rosalie. There's a small runway here.'

'No, Freddie, I'm sure I'll be fine after a short rest and I don't want to be a pain.'

'You're being a pain by refusing my suggestions.' He softened his words with another grin. 'Now sit.'

She watched him go, guilt, gratitude and some other emotion too close to the love she was trying hard to suppress rising up within her. She didn't want to ruin this trip for him. But then she hadn't anticipated feeling like this. Here she was in new surroundings, feeling like she'd been tossed off a vicious fairground ride without the candy floss and the hot dogs to fuel it.

And that thought really didn't help.

She took Freddie's advice and dropped onto the sand, sucked in a deep breath and blew it out slowly, her eyes going to the unmoving horizon and feeling marginally better for it. She just needed the ground beneath her to stop moving and all would be well. A few more deep breaths and—

Her phone buzzed from the depths of her straw bag. She frowned and reached inside to pull it out. It was Sadie in their group chat.

Where's our update? Waiting (im)patiently... x

She smiled at the screen in spite of the continued rocking and the knowledge that soon the trip would be over and if Freddie didn't change his mind, they would be going their separate ways.

She tapped in her reply.

Paradise is just that. Paradise x

Sadie's response was instant.

Never mind paradise, what's he like? Xxx

He's...

She stopped typing.

What could she say? She could hardly reveal it was Freddie. She'd considered messaging them the very first night, but every scenario of her offloading the truth resulted in a barrage of questions and very likely phone calls too and she didn't want the chaos of it. Not now when time wasn't on their side.

She also wasn't ready to face their potential wrath. Though they would mean well, their anger stemming from their love for her, they really weren't going to take the news lightly. Part of the whole M thing was about putting Freddie behind her and instead it had done the total opposite.

It had been enough of a shock dealing with it herself. Telling them and dealing with their reactions too…

No, that discussion could wait for her return to Edinburgh. Until then she would make the most of this. Paradise and Freddie.

…perfect x

She sent it. It was the truth after all.
Izzy replied first.

How exciting! M made good on their promise then? xxx

Sadie came next, in true Sadie fashion.

You'd hope so when they charge all those zeroes! But when we're talking perfect, how perfect? Like the full Mr Perfect package—eight-pack ripped, drop-dead gorgeous and a brain? Cos he needs a brain to be with you, Ms Clever Clogs! Mwah!

She laughed at her friend's bluntness and instantly regretted it. Her body really wasn't ready for laughter.

Dragging in a breath, she looked over her shoulder to where her Mr Perfect was now chatting animatedly to their tour guide. He was wearing a white V-neck T-shirt and navy board shorts today, the outfit simple, but on him…even with the churning sensation still underway, her body pulsed with heat. He definitely was her Mr Perfect.

Their tour guide was frowning and nodding at whatever Freddie was saying and her ears burned. He was no doubt telling him how sick she felt, how she hadn't been able to cope with the crossing and was now ruining the day for all of them.

Well, no, he wouldn't be saying that last bit, that was all her as she blamed herself.

Slipping her hand beneath her cap, she rubbed at her forehead and wished the sensation away, but it was no good. She couldn't force her body to toe the line and behave, no matter how much she wanted it to.

Her phone buzzed and she squinted at the screen, Sadie's message blared back at her.

Well???

She pursed her lips and typed.

Yes, he has a brain! And, yes, he has a body you would approve of. He is perfect for me xx

She grimaced. A bit too honest, perhaps… But it was just what her friends would want to hear. Sadie replied.

Oh, man, I'm so jealous.

Then Izzy.

You change your men as often as you change your underwear, Sadie, you don't get to be jealous!

Sadie again:

Do not.

Izzy:

Do so.

And now it was her friends sending her dizzy. She groaned and dropped back onto the sand, not caring that her hair was still wet from the waves hitting the catamaran and that the sand would cling to it.

Her phone continued to buzz, and she lifted it against the sun and tapped in a message.

How old are you two again?

Sadie replied.

Not as old as you.

Then Izzy:

You really need to learn to mince your words, S!

Sadie:

That's not how the saying goes, and anyway life's too short. Which is why I'm over the moon you've found your man. So, do we get a name at least?

She bit her bottom lip.

You'll have to wait until I get back.

Sadie:

Which is when?

Izzy:

Give her a break, she doesn't want to think about home already!

Sadie:

Izzy, shh!

She thought it over. By her reckoning, if all went to plan, she would be back in Edinburgh Saturday lunchtime and going home to an empty penthouse...

She replied.

Saturday lunchtime xx

Sadie:

Sunday brunch, then?

An afternoon and night alone with her thoughts? No, thank you. The spasm to her gut wasn't so much the gift of the sea now, and she clutched her hand to it.

'You okay?'

She jumped at Freddie's husky voice so close and angled her head back. He was right behind her, a silhouette against the sun.

She covered her eyes and blinked up at him. 'Just catching up with my friends.'

'I meant your stomach.' He gestured to where

she clutched her belly and she wondered how he'd feel if she confessed that he was the cause of that particular gesture.

'Hopefully I will be soon. What did our guide say?'

Her phone vibrated in her hand and she looked at the screen. It was Sadie.

???

Then Izzy:

Give the girl a second at least...

'Sorry I just need to sign off and then I'm all yours.'

She sensed his body pulse over her accidental innuendo, and her cheeks flushed—it beat pale and sickly, though.

She tapped out her reply, trying to concentrate on it while her body flooded with salacious warmth.

Saturday night would be better. If you can?

She dropped in a fingers-crossed emoji and added prayer hands too for good measure.

Sadie:

It's a date! I'll cook!

Izzy:

No, I'll cook, you can bring the wine x

Sadie:

Much better plan.

She smiled, feeling their support across the miles, and signed off.

See you then, loves xxx

She popped her phone back into her bag and made to sit up.

'As you were,' Freddie commanded softly. 'I'll join you.'

'You'll get sand everywhere.'

'Ah, yes, the joy of sand.' He sank down beside her and lay back, his hand reaching to cover hers. It was such a comforting gesture, so natural and easy. It felt like it meant something and no amount of trying to rationalise it away as just a thoughtful gesture between old friends was working.

'This stuff is like talcum powder anyway.' He used his other hand to scoop up a handful and she watched as he let it fall through his fingers.

'And when was the last time you came up close and personal with talc?'

She lifted her gaze to his and her heart gave a

little leap. The sun glinted off his dark hair, the tanned glow to his skin making his blue eyes even more vibrant and highlighting the chiselled angle of his cheekbones, his jaw, and every breath she now took captured his scent...

'You'd be surprised. My sister thinks it's very important to thrust uncle duties on me at every opportunity when I visit home.'

She smiled, the idea of seeing him in that role warming her heart all the more. 'How lovely.'

'If you say so. James is two but what he lacks in age he makes up for in noise. He'll make a fine Highgrove.'

'Though he won't be a Highgrove, will he?'

'He is.'

'Oh, I would have thought he'd have his father's name. I shouldn't have assumed in this day and—'

'He does have his father's name,' he interjected, tension bracketing his mouth. 'But he's still a Highgrove without the name.'

'I just— I mean...' Her voice trailed off as she realised she was pressing him into a conversation that could only spell trouble.

'You're talking titles. You're talking about my child. My heir. The heir I won't ever have because I have no intention of marrying.'

She swallowed, the pang in her chest too great. 'Yes.'

He said nothing, his eyes on the sky so very pensive.

'Have you considered what happens to the line if you don't?'

Why was she even pressing him on this? Did she hope he would suddenly turn around to her and say, 'Hey, let's forget the last ten years ever happened and get married like we always planned, have a home, kids, a dog.'

Wasn't going to happen.

But…

His eyes flitted to her briefly. Did he see it all in her face? Was that why he'd looked away again so quickly?

'My sister has another child on the way, and likely another after that. There will be no end of possible heirs if she carries on the way she is.'

He offered her a smile but it left her feeling dead inside, her heart breaking as she thought of Freddie never having a family of his own. Yes, if it couldn't be with her, she didn't want to imagine it being with someone else. But to always be alone, to never have kids when it had been his dream when they had been younger. Had she ruined him so much?

The question that left her was far safer: 'When is she due?'

His brows drew together. 'Hmm?'

'You said your sister has another on the way…'

'Oh, yes.' Another smile softened his brow. 'In a couple of months.'

'Wow, so soon?'

He chuckled. 'Now you sound like my father.'

'Not your mother, though. I bet she's in her element.'

'You've got that right.' He went quiet again, withdrawing into his thoughts, and she watched as his lips quirked with whatever they were.

'They make good grandparents,' he said eventually, his tone sombre. 'Better grandparents than parents in many ways.'

She swallowed the little lump that formed in her throat. 'How so?'

'They're more relaxed. Mum's been trying to get Dad home more over the years and he finally seems to be paying attention. You should see him at Christmas now. He's practically regressed into being the biggest kid of all.'

She covered his hand on top of hers. 'Christmas was always very special at Highgrove.'

The manor would be lit up with decorations, festive colour in every room, the scent too. She'd spend the entire holiday season buzzing around the house with Freddie, trying not to get underfoot but getting involved all the same.

'It had its moments.' He turned to look at her, his smile not quite reaching the wistful look in his eyes. 'We had some good times.'

She nodded. 'We had *lots* of good times.'

So much passed between them in a simple look, so many memories. Her mother would always work late into the night, helping with the parties in the run-up to Christmas, ensuring every need was catered for, so they had been free to do what they'd wanted. Sneak mulled wine, eggnog, mince pies from Maggie, whatever had taken their fancy. All those good years of being friends, and then the one year when they had been more, so much more. Engaged and ostracised in one.

'I didn't go back to Highgrove, not even for Christmas, for a long time afterwards,' Freddie said as he travelled the same road as her. 'It took a lot of persuasion from Ally to get me back there, and even then four years had passed. I'd graduated, started a new life...'

'Really?' She frowned. 'But—but Christmas was such a huge thing for your family. It was so important for you all to be together.'

He looked away, withdrawing from her and she clutched his hand tighter.

'Freddie?'

'I told you, I blamed them. I didn't want to know my parents after they forced you out.'

'They did it because they loved you,' she said quietly. 'It must have broken their hearts to have you gone for so long.'

'What about my heart, Jas?' The force of his words made her flinch as he turned to her. 'And how can you lie there and defend them, after everything they said and did?'

'I'm not.'

'You are.'

'I'm just saying I understand, even if it hurt, even if—'

'Even if it tore us apart.'

Her breath shuddered through her and she looked at the sky.

'Sorry...' he said suddenly, squeezing her fingers. 'I've come to terms with it, but...'

'It still hurts.'

He nodded and she gave him a sad smile as she added, 'It still hurts us both.'

His eyes searched hers, taking in her words, accepting them. 'It's a ten-year-old pain, it makes sense that we can't simply shut it off.'

'I know.' She breathed in deeply as she gazed into the eyes of the man she loved so much, the man she'd missed so much... The man who deserved a family of his own to love and to cherish and with whom to continue on all the wondrous Highgrove traditions.

'It's a shame you're so set against marriage, Freddie, because you'd make a wonderful father.'

It may have come out of left field, in his eyes anyway, but she hadn't been able to keep it trapped inside and it was worth the flicker of emotion in his face, the pulse of his fingers beneath hers. Because for that brief moment she knew she'd opened his eyes to it and the joy of possibility.

But then he shook his head, his expression morphing into one of incredulity. 'So I can adopt the same parenting technique my father did for all those years? No, thank you.'

'Technique?' she frowned. 'What do you mean?'

'Absent parenting.' His eyes were on the sky again. 'I often thought the only reason he'd had a child was to produce an heir, someone to pass everything on to. When I was younger he was never around, when I was older all he wanted to discuss was the estate, the business…'

'But he loves you, Freddie.'

He shrugged it off. 'Either I was invisible or I was an asset. He only had Ally to keep Mum happy, to keep her occupied, give her less free time to call on his.'

'I'm sure that's not—'

'Hey, it's okay, Red.' He turned to her. 'I'm over it and, like I say, things are different now. Dad's improving with age, just like a fine wine…'

He was trying to make light of it, but she wasn't having it. 'Freddie, don't joke!'

'I'm not. I'm being serious. Being a grandparent has changed him.'

She stared at him, struggling to find the words.

'And he taught me my most important lesson.'

'Which is?'

'That I make a great uncle. A father…not so much.'

She didn't stop staring at him, her heart caught in a desperate spiral. 'Do you honestly think that because your father was an absent parent, you would be too?'

'Why wouldn't I? I'm just as busy, I'll be more so when I take on the estate, the title. I'll be stepping into his shoes and then some.'

'But you've also learned from his mistakes.'

'I've learnt to avoid them…and before you say it, this isn't the kind of avoidance that needs rectifying, Jas.'

'Of course it is, Freddie! This is worse than not standing up to your parents over the years.' He went to reply, but she wasn't done. 'Having a family of your own, being the good father I *know* you would be…you can't not do that!'

His eyes narrowed but he said nothing, and she could see the doubt, the sadness, the disbelief that he could be something different, something better.

'You're nothing like your father, Freddie… Okay, you look a little like him, and sometimes you can definitely be as brooding and pig-headed,' she teased, and saw the glimmer of a sparkle in his eyes. 'But your heart is your biggest asset. Yes, I love your brains…' *stay clear of the L word*, came the warning but she pressed on anyway '…and your intelligence. You don't look half bad either.'

She rolled onto her side, forcing back the sudden wave of seasickness and the rocking of the entire world as she rested her hand over his heart. 'But when you love, you love with the whole of you. You could never be like your father was, because it's not in you to be that way.'

He held her gaze, quiet, contemplative, and she let her eyes tell him what was in her heart, how she meant every word. Meant it and wanted it… for them.

Baby steps. That's what this was. Baby steps into doing what Madison had advised and getting him to see how good it could be if he opened his eyes to it. To an 'us'.

The problem was that her own heart was opening up right along with it and if she couldn't convince him, if this week truly was to be it…

She shut the thought down and lowered her head to his chest, curled into his side. She had to try, though…

'It's a shame you're so set against marriage, Freddie, because you'd make a wonderful father.'

Her words echoed through him long after their rest on the beach, but the jeering inner laughter that had brushed off her statement as crazy was gradually softening. Hours later, as they trekked through the rainforest and he was supposed to be focusing on what they were seeing, he could feel the change underway inside. The change tugging him back to how he'd once been, the future so bright and filled with promise. The promise of exactly that: a wife, kids, a home in Scotland.

And not just any wife—Jasmine.

It would be so easy to follow that path again, to let her wrap him up in her warmth, her light, her…love.

But then what?

His parents' expectations hadn't changed, the view of their peers hadn't changed. He'd be dragging her back into their elitist world where they would as readily snub her now as they had back then. Could their relationship truly survive it? Survive and flourish? With children *and* all the demands on their time from their respective businesses, his charity, the estate? He could feel his heart racing away with him, and not in a good way.

But if Jasmine was willing to face it, to risk it…

You're getting all fanciful, came the warning. *You haven't had a relationship that lasted more than a month in ten years, why would now be any different?*

Because it was her. It was Jasmine. And she'd made him remember how good it felt to be with someone, the right someone.

But what if it wasn't? What if this only worked now because they were away from all the obstacles that stopped them from having a life together before? What if they risked it now and…?

'Oh, my goodness, Freddie!' Her giddy call cut through his thoughts and he looked at her in the distance, her cheeks all bright again and jutting into her sunglasses as she grinned at him.

For the briefest moment he just treasured the colour being back in her cheeks, her body free of the tension that had held her taut on the boat. He'd wanted so badly to take away her discomfort, he'd wanted to be able to do something, anything…and it was just seasickness, nothing life threatening, but he'd felt so helpless in his desperation.

As helpless as he was in controlling the way he felt around her. The way he felt *for* her.

Day four of seven and she had his world turned upside down. All over again.

He quashed the anxious churn in his gut and grinned at her, grateful that his sunglasses would hide the rest.

'You have to see these, Freddie!'

He picked his way through the dense rainforest to join her and Michel, their guide.

'Welcome to the star of our tour!' Michel chuckled up at him. He was a small man with a big personality. 'This is the *coco de mer*—the coconut of the sea.'

'Look at them, Freddie! Just look!' Jasmine gestured to the ground. 'They look like giant…well, you know…'

She made a gesture like she was massaging a long, curved cylinder—she couldn't mean… He eyed the thick phallic object on the ground, with its small, yellow star-like flowers dotted around it and his grin widened. Oh, yes, she did.

'That is the catkin of the male tree,' Michel explained.

Jasmine gave a little giggle. 'It would be the male, wouldn't it?'

'And *you* would make that remark,' Freddie teased, high on her playfulness as their tour guide laughed heartily.

'Can you blame me? Look at what the female tree produces, it looks like a giant bottom!' She squeezed her fingers together like they held invisible sponges, as if he needed reminding of what one looked like, and then bent to lift a hefty wooden-looking thing off the ground. 'Goodness! It weighs a ton!'

'Yes, the nut or seed of the female tree can actually weigh up to twenty kilograms, if not more,' Michel informed them.

She turned and presented it to Freddie. 'See!'

His cheeks ached with his continued grin. It did indeed look like a very round bottom.

'And you turn it around and it has hair, just *there*!' Jasmine really was suppressing her giggles now and he felt light inside, caught up in her happy aura, her healthy glow, the boat all but forgotten along with his worries of moments before.

'The nut can grow to be as big as half a metre and they come out of the husks you see there.' Michel pointed up to the palms towering above them and the bulbous green orbs hanging there. 'It is the largest seed in the plant kingdom and is very rare, found only in the Seychelles, on the islands of Praslin and Curieuse.'

'Impressive!' She passed it to Freddie. 'Here, cop a feel.'

His laugh burst out of him as he shook his head at her and did just as she asked. 'Very smooth.'

She laughed more.

'You're such a kid.'

'Takes one to know one.' She winked at him and bent to put it back on the ground, ensuring he got an extended view of another bottom entirely and one that he definitely did want to feel. Not that he would in front of their guide. But later... definitely later.

'Because of the unusual qualities to both,' Michel continued, 'many a legend has been told about these trees.'

'Oh, yes...' she sent Freddie a look '...we can imagine.'

'For example, it is believed that at night, when storms rage, the trees come together in a passionate embrace.'

She clasped her hands to her chest. 'How romantic!'

'Indeed. But as they are shy, legend also has it that should you catch them at it, you will go blind or quite possibly die.'

'Well, that's depressing!' she blurted, her pout dramatic.

Freddie chuckled. He wasn't sure what was

more entertaining, Jasmine's reaction—which he really, really did want to kiss off her face—or the tale itself. Either way, he knew he had to capture this moment.

He stepped back, pulled his phone from the pocket of his shorts.

'I assume they're not too shy to have a photo taken?' he said to Michel.

'Ah, of course, but let me get one of you together instead?'

Jasmine's smile faltered on her lips. Her thoughts were probably mirroring his own. Getting a photo of her had been risky enough, a permanent memory for him to take with him when this was all over, but a photo of them together...

He offered the phone to Michel, who took it from him and waved them closer together. 'Closer, a bit more. Do you want to pick up the catkin and the nut?'

Jasmine let out a giggle, her mood lifting as easily as that. 'Get the catkin, Freddie! I'll do the bottom!'

He bent and picked it up. It was impossible not to hold it in a way that *wasn't* suggestive, and Jasmine's body quivered with her continued laughter as she clutched the nut to her front.

He shook his head at her, hooked his arm around her waist to pull her close, inhaled her scent, her giddiness...looked at the camera.

'Say coconut of the sea!' Michel ordered, and

they performed for the camera, Freddie's grin very easy when he had his arm around a laughing Jasmine.

It felt so right. So perfect.

And now he would have the photo to remind him of this moment, again and again and again.

Michel handed the phone back to him, his grin turning mischievous, his wink definitely so. 'It is also said that the meat of the nut has powerful aphrodisiac qualities.'

Jasmine leaned in closer. 'Fancy that, Freddie.'

He shook his head again. He didn't need an aphrodisiac when Jasmine was around. He was tuned in, turned on and more alive than he'd felt in years.

Ten, to be exact.

And soon it would be over once more. Unless…

Should he listen to her? Could they give it a shot? A real shot. Take it slowly, day by day. They didn't have to test their relationship at the outset with all that it meant to be a Highgrove. There was time to adjust to the idea, for his family to adjust too, before throwing the responsibilities and social pressures of being a Highgrove into the mix. He could stay in New York a little longer, they could commute, date, see the world. Long-distance relationships worked all the time… didn't they?

He tightened his arm around her, kissed her head, his heart pressing him to agree. 'Let's see what else the Vallée de Mai has to offer before you get any more excited...'

'*Moi?*' She turned to pout up at him, her nut jutting against his catkin. 'You forget how well I can read you, Freddie.'

She gifted him another wink before placing the nut back on the ground and taking off after Michel, leaving Freddie, his catkin and his racing thoughts hanging.

CHAPTER THIRTEEN

JASMINE LET OUT a squeal of delight and squeezed her legs tighter around Freddie's waist as he swirled her reclining body around in the sea, his grin as bright as the sun.

'I could get used to this,' she said as she relaxed into the move and let him take the lead.

'You and me both.' He tugged her up against his chest and she wrapped her arms around him, kissing him with all the pleasure his words had triggered.

It was day five. They barely had any time left. There would be no getting used to anything if she couldn't change his mind.

He ran his hands through her hair, held her close as he broke the kiss to stare down into her eyes.

'What?' she said, sensing something coming, seeing it swim in his breathtaking blue eyes and spasm in his jaw.

He pressed his forehead to hers, squeezed his eyes shut with a small shake of his head before opening them again. 'Nothing.'

She raised her brows, toying with the damp hair at his nape. 'You could have fooled me.'

'I was treasuring the moment, treasuring you in this teasing slip of a red bikini.' He rolled his body against hers suggestively, but she knew he was trying to distract her from the true nature of his thoughts. 'Is that a crime?'

'No.' She kissed him sweetly. 'I'm treasuring it too. I wish it didn't have to end.'

'All good things have to come to an end, Jas. That's life and why it needs to be treasured now.'

'But this…' She caught her lip in her teeth, searched his eyes that seemed to tell her so much and yet nothing at all. She needed to be brave. She needed to be honest and confident and strong. All the things she wished she'd been ten years ago. He may not want to get all serious right now, but she did. 'This doesn't have to end.'

She felt the tension seeping into his body. 'Reality has other ideas.'

'You mean your family do,' she said softly.

'Ten years hasn't changed anything, Jas. They still expect a high society bride.'

'But you don't want that.'

He wet his lips, hesitant. Was it a chink in his armour? Was she slowly getting through to him? 'No, I don't.'

'But…?' she pressed, knowing the risk she was taking, that she could be destroying the moment, and potentially the rest of the stay too if she called it wrong. But she wouldn't be afraid. Not this time.

'If life was simple, I wouldn't hesitate to go after the future you seem so sure is possible, but don't you want more? You deserve better than to be surrounded by a family like mine.'

She laughed to hide the sea of emotion inside her. 'I deserve better, and yet I'm the one deemed to be lacking.'

'You know what I mean.'

'I do, Freddie, but I'm not interested in running away. Not any more.'

'You say that like you've forgotten how it was...' He suddenly looked grey in the sun. His blue eyes were pale and haunted, his arms wrapping around her, holding her close. 'Do you not remember how they were? What they said? And the people that witnessed it, your mother included?'

Her lashes fluttered as the memory chilled her heart. 'Of course I remember.'

'I'm sorry, I don't want to inflict any more pain, Jas.' He gritted his teeth, his throat bobbing as his arms flexed around her.

'Don't apologise.' She cupped his face, speared his eyes with her own as she stressed, 'It's all in the past. What I care about is the future, Freddie. The future we could have if we choose it.'

She reached up to press a kiss to his lips, a moment's connection before she dropped back.

'Don't you see, Freddie, we've spent the last ten years filling our days, our nights too, trying to find contentment.'

'And failed.'

'Yes.'

'Because something was always missing.'

She nodded. 'We didn't have each other.'

His smile was small, but they were finishing each other's sentences, which had to be a good sign. It had to mean he was feeling the same way...

'Don't you want to at least try?'

He took a deep breath, his eyes not once leaving hers. 'I'd like to think we could try, but there are so many factors to consider.'

'Like your family?'

'Eventually, yes. But I was thinking more of our work, my charity, our crazy schedules.'

'Isn't the perk of getting to the heights we have that we get to ease off a little now and bring in more people to help, share the load? My mother tried to tell me the same, even in the early days when Work Made Simple was just taking off, Tim too, but my app was my passion then...'

'And now?'

She gave a small laugh. 'You never used to be such a compliment seeker!'

'Not the words I want to hear, Red...' He bowed his head, kissed her deeply, so deeply she almost lost sight of the magnitude of where their conversation was heading.

She pushed him away. 'You're my passion, Freddie. Happy?'

'Very.' His grin took her breath away, but the

tension was far too quick to follow. 'How do you feel about a long-distance relationship?'

She frowned. 'But I'm in Edinburgh, and so will you—'

He was shaking his head, killing off her words.

'No. If we do this, I'll delay my return, give us time to date, to do all the things we never had the money, the freedom, to do before. Have a relationship away from the pressures of Highgrove. Give us time to see where this goes on our terms.'

'But you said they needed you to come home, your father, the estate, Rupert…'

'They've waited this long, they can wait a little longer.'

Her frown deepened, hope and relief warring with what was expected of him, what was needed of him in Edinburgh, of his sister, his nephew… Was she coming between them again?

'But—'

'I'm not talking for ever, Red, just until we're ready.'

Was he right? Did they need to take this time now before facing the pressures that had broken them so long ago?

But how would they know when they were ready? She couldn't imagine feeling any more ready than she did right now.

'Hey, don't look so pensive! I thought you'd be pleased, happy. I don't want to be all egotistical about it, but I'd even go as far as to say overjoyed…' He spun her in the water, eased her body up against him until her eyes were at the same level as his. 'What say you, Red?'

Happiness had her chest blooming so much she thought it would burst. 'I am happy, so happy.'

She kissed him, wrapped her arms around his neck tightly, scarcely daring to believe and believing all the same. Pushing out the worry with the strength to follow his lead this time.

'This calls for a drink to celebrate,' he said against her lips.

'*Another* toast?'

He laughed. 'Yes!'

'Come on.' He released her, taking hold of her hand as he turned away.

But she held still. 'I'll follow you in a second.'

'Okay.' He eyed her speculatively. 'Though you are starting to look rather prune-like so I wouldn't leave it too long.'

'Freddie!' She thrust water at him, her laugh high. High on their conversation, on the future, on him, all him.

But the truth was that she needed a moment. Her heart was drumming a crazy beat, her insides alive with a thousand flutters, and she needed to catch her breath. Clear her thoughts.

He chuckled. 'Suit yourself, but don't be too long. I have plans for today and all of them involve you, champagne and whatever creole delights Monique can have delivered to our room.'

'You're insatiable!'

'So are you, my love…'

My love. Her racing heart pulsed.

'Just another of the many reasons we're our perfect match.'

He winked and turned away. Leaving her floating on air rather than water. She watched him wade back towards the deck that reached out over the sea, the rich timber platform creating a seamless connection between their bedroom quarters and the water, and sucked in the deepest of breaths. She wanted to cry out to the heavens in joy, dance on the spot, somersault, do all manner of crazy things to ease the chaos inside her.

But it wasn't chaos, it was a fullness. A rich warmth where there'd once been a chill, an emptiness. A Freddie-shaped hole.

She gave a little squeal, unable to keep it all contained, and turned to dive beneath the surface of the water, enjoying the rush of it cooling off her flushed face. She and Freddie. Freddie and her. It was happening.

She surfaced and rolled onto her back, floating in the water that was so very calm today. Much better than yesterday morning when they'd taken the trip out to Praslin. The memory of it made her smile, even as she touched a hand to her stomach, grateful that the sensation was long gone. But Freddie had been so desperate to look after her, to make her feel better, because he loved her. He hadn't said it yet, but then neither had she. They hadn't needed to. It was there in their words, their faces, as obvious as it had ever been.

Something nudged her foot, and she flinched away, looking to see what it was.

Wow!

Now, *that* was a turtle!

Not one from Freddie's imaginary spiel to keep her distracted on the boat, but a real, bona fide hawksbill, its brightly coloured, intricately patterned shell so beautiful as it glided through the water around her. It wasn't scared of her or wary. It was such a pleasure to watch. The only thing that could make the moment more perfect would be if Freddie were by her side.

She looked towards the shore, trying to seek him out and gesture to him. She frowned, shaded her eyes from the sun as she searched the deck, the room… There he was, in the bedroom. Her frown deepened.

He was pacing, his phone to his ear as he raked his hand through his hair and clutched the back of his head.

She forgot the turtle, forgot the beautiful water.

Something was wrong.

Something was very wrong.

'No. It's fine,' he told his sister firmly. 'I'll be there as soon as I can.'

'Freddie?'

He turned to see Jasmine behind him, the lurch inside his chest so forceful that he had to press the phone to his ear to avoid dropping it altogether. Her green eyes were drawn with concern, her knuckles white where she gripped her fluffy cream towel around her.

He tried to give a reassuring smile, but it was stiff, fraught with the news his sister had just shared. Fraught with the realisation that their time together was over sooner than planned. More than that, they were over. What an idiot he'd been to think they could have time to build a relationship on their terms, under their control, cushioned from the destructive forces of his family, their peers, the demands on his time.

'I'll call you as soon as I have an ETA, Ally.'

He hung up and strode to the bed, tossing the phone down on it and trying to quash the rolling of his gut, the hammering of his heart, his mind awash with what was happening back home and what it meant.

He sensed rather than heard Jasmine move, her fingers soft as they came to rest on his shoulder.

'What's happened?' Her voice was so quiet and all he wanted to do, all he ever wanted to do, was pull her into his arms and hold her close. He didn't want to leave. He didn't want to go it alone. Not any more.

But this… He wasn't ready, *they* weren't ready. But he had no choice. The very reason he had to go was the very reason he couldn't take her with him. His family. His father. They needed him. Not in a year or two's time. Now.

'Freddie?' she whispered, her body gently coming up against his back, comforting him when he didn't deserve to take comfort from her. Not when he knew what he was about to do would crush her. That off the back of their very recent conversation he was about to take it all back.

He turned, tried to prepare himself for seeing her this close, and still his breath left him, his arms wrapping around her and holding her close as he sucked in a stabilising breath. And another.

Again, not fair. Not fair to take strength from her presence when…

'I have to go. My father— My father's had a stroke.'

'Oh, Freddie!' Her head shot up, her green eyes piercing his tortured soul. How could it be that the one woman he wanted to get him through this was the one he couldn't have by his side? 'I'm so sorry. Is he…is he okay?'

'I don't know. He's stable but…' He released her, ran his hands through his hair, panic rising. 'They're running tests and I need to be there.'

'Of course you do.' She wrapped her arms around her middle, her eyes blazing with her compassion, her concern. 'What can I do?'

'Nothing.' She flinched and he cursed his abruptness, thrust his hands back through his hair.

'I'm going to make some calls. See what flights I can sort.'

'Let me do that.'

'No, it's fine. My PA will take care of most it.'

'Then tell me what else I can do. Anything?'

He shook his head. What he wanted he wouldn't—*couldn't*—ask for.

'There's nothing. Just— I'm sorry.'

'Why are you apologising?'

He looked her straight in the eye, forced the words out. 'For leaving.'

She shook her head. 'You don't need to apologise for that, you need to get home.'

'I don't just mean... I don't— I can't...'

'Freddie?' She frowned up at him. 'You can't...?'

'This changes things, Jas, don't you see?' His head was a jumbled mess, his words too.

'Things? What things?'

'There's no time any more, no time for us before I return to Highgrove.'

'No. But that's okay. I can still come with you. You shouldn't go through this alone. I wouldn't come to the hospital, not with... I wouldn't want to cause distress, but I could be in Edinburgh for you.'

She stepped towards him, and he reached out on impulse, his hands soft on her hips. She was offering him everything in that second and the selfish part of him, the part that had longed for her all this time, the part that had been elated on the plans forming not thirty minutes ago, wanted to say yes.

Say yes, and never look back. But he couldn't. He couldn't see a way to that, not now.

'I can't ask that of you.'

'Of course you can,' she whispered.

She was so small, so petite, and he was transported back ten years. To the same small frame, facing a room full of his parents' nearest and dearest, the laughter in their eyes, the sympathy in some, the scorn in others. No. Never again.

'No, Jas. You should stay and enjoy the rest of your holiday. You work hard, you're supposed to play harder, right?'

He forced a smile, tried to act like his whole world wasn't falling in.

'Don't, Freddie. Don't act like this is all okay, because it's not okay. We were making a commitment to one another... We were making plans.'

'Plans that can no longer happen.'

'So we'll make new plans. We'll work out another path to keep us together.'

Her words teased at his shattering heart, tugged at his chest, and he had to stop them, stop her, stop it.

He pressed a kiss to her lips, a long, desperate kiss to get enough, enough to see him through, and she let him take, her body turning into liquid in his hands...and maybe, just maybe... No!

He thrust her away, tried to ignore the way her body trembled beneath his fingers, the way she shook her head at him, the way her dazed eyes glistened with realisation. This was goodbye. It was over.

'You've had a shock, Freddie, a huge shock, you're not thinking clearly.'

'I'm thinking well enough to know I can't do it. I can't deal with you, us, Dad, my family, all of it!' He'd crashed to earth the second his sister had given him the news. The brutal reality of life hitting him smack in the face and laughing at the very idea he could have had a future on his own terms. 'We were foolish to see this as some fantastical second chance when the reality is so very different.'

'It doesn't have to be all that different, not if we don't want it to be.'

He hesitated, staring into those dizzying green eyes and wishing so hard he could believe it. But he'd gone it alone for so many years and alone he could keep control of his life, his heart. He couldn't inflict pain, neither could he suffer it.

And yet here they both were swimming in it. Pain.

Not even a week in and this was where they were. How would it be weeks, months, a year down the line?

He couldn't listen, couldn't even look at her. He needed this over and he needed to be back in

Scotland. At his father's bedside. The man had always been a towering strength, a force to be reckoned with, now he lay vulnerable, weak…

'I'm sorry.' He turned away from her, shutting it all out, something he'd become a master of over the years, and snatched up his phone, dialling his PA. 'Please go, Jas. Let me deal with this. I'll come and find you once I have my flight sorted.'

He sensed her step towards him and stilled, his entire body rigid as he anticipated her touch… But nothing came.

She padded from the room as stealthily as she'd made her way into his heart again and he clenched his eyes shut, forced down the rising tide within him.

Focus on Dad, on your family who need you.

The rest can come later, much later…when she's no longer within reach.

CHAPTER FOURTEEN

JASMINE POURED THE wine as Sadie and Izzy debated the complicated state of her love life. Now that they'd got over the shock of M choosing Freddie as her perfect match, they were rapidly debating her next move.

Like it was some complicated game of chess. Not a star-crossed love affair that had survived the test of years and come back all the stronger for it. All the stronger but with no hope of a future.

Because if there had been, Freddie would have wanted her by his side in his hour of need. If she'd had the option of having him by her side when she'd lost Mum, she would have grabbed hold with both hands.

'You know, I still can't believe it was Freddie Highgrove,' Izzy murmured into her freshly filled glass.

'It's all very romantic.' Sadie swooned dramatically as she flopped back onto the living room floor, her glass safely resting on the coffee table. 'Very fated.'

'Yes, we've done the whole fated thing to death already,' Jasmine grumbled. 'It doesn't make me feel any better.'

'Well, of course not.' Sadie shot up onto her elbows to stare at Jasmine perched on the edge of her teal sofa. 'You're in love and broken-hearted all over again! It's ridiculous.'

'I'm so glad the state of my heart is something to ridicule.'

'I wasn't ridiculing it.'

'You just said it was ridiculous.'

'Yes, well, it is,' she blustered. 'He should have taken you with him.'

'Yes, he should have,' Izzy added softly, from the other end of the sofa. 'But…not many people would react to the news he'd just been given in a sane, rational way. He was clearly out of his mind with worry, and to have your very new, very uncertain relationship on top… It's kind of understandable.'

'Yeah, yeah, I get it.' Sadie nodded vigorously. 'And I hate to say it after all these years and us telling you to forget him, Jas, but I feel sorry for him. And you. It's quite obvious he's hopelessly in love with you.'

'Is it?' Jasmine took up her glass and threw back too big a sip. She couldn't help it. Her friends were a bad influence and as for Freddie…it had been days, days and not a word. Not that they'd exchanged numbers, but she knew Freddie could reach her if he really wanted to. M would make sure of that. 'I don't know how you can think that, not when I'm struggling to believe it.'

'Don't be ridiculous.'

She gave Sadie a hard stare.

'Okay, no more ridiculous. Help me out, Iz!'

'From what you've told us, I have to say I'm with Sadie. I think he loves you and he's protecting you, protecting both of you from the past repeating itself.'

'Exactly!' Sadie declared.

'But we dealt with all that, we were making plans—'

'Plans that kept things in your control,' Izzy said softly. 'Gave you time together before facing such a huge hurdle.'

'He basically panicked, Jas, surely you can see that?'

'I thought so too, at the time, but he's not reached out, not even the briefest of messages.'

'He has a lot on his plate.'

She grimaced. She knew that too and now she felt even worse for questioning it.

'And it's not like you've messaged him.'

'No, but I wanted to give him the space he so obviously wanted.'

'Well, he's had his space!' Sadie blustered. 'Time to close in.'

'Hey, easy, Sades…' Izzy waved their excitable friend down. 'The thing is he's so clearly used to going it alone and keeping a tight lid on his life. The whole talk of planning, taking things slowly, putting off the inevitable showdown with his family and facing his aristocratic world that treated you like…well, crap. And then life comes along and turns all those plans for a future on their head. I get why he walked away from you—he was protecting you from a future so out of his control it scared him.'

'But I don't need his protection, I want us to face it together.'

'Maybe part of him feels that the old Jasmine is still in there deep down, the one that did run in the face of his parents all those years ago,' Sadie supplied, trying to be helpful, but it only frustrated her more.

'I told you, we dealt with all that. And he knows I'm different now, he knows I'm stronger, better equipped to deal with it.' She cursed in her desperation. 'I'm a successful businesswoman, able to stand up in front of thousands and fight for what I believe in, so why would he doubt my ability to stand and fight for us now?'

'Because the risk is far greater.' Izzy gave a hapless shrug.

'Absolutely.' Sadie nodded. 'If he was to believe in you now, and you broke his heart, or worse, if he believed in you and his parents, their world broke you all over again when you are, as you say, a strong, successful, independent businesswoman…'

Her stomach lurched as her friends' meaning hit home. They were right, there was so much more to this. So much more for him to fret over, to worry about, to doubt. Even if he had put their past to bed.

'It's true, honey, think about it,' Izzy urged softly.

Jasmine's brain was racing.

After the initial shock of his leaving the Seychelles, she'd gone over and over everything. Revisiting every conversation, every look. Questioning whether she'd imagined the love shining back at her, the desire to be together, the happiness. Was there a part of him that didn't want to let her in? To share his life? Was it an excuse to end it?

No, she couldn't believe it of him. He was hurting and acting on impulse, pushing her out and doing what he was used to, shouldering it alone. And this in itself was a test, a test she had to win. To prove that this time she was staying. She wouldn't run like she once had, she would stay by his side, where she wanted to be and where she should be. 'I need to show him we're stronger together.'

'Ooh, fighting talk,' Sadie cooed. 'I like it!'

'Only…what if he won't give me the chance?'

Izzy frowned. 'Why does he need to give you the chance?'

'Since when do you wait for an opportunity to come your way? You need to take the bull by the horns,' Sadie said, doing an impression of doing just that with her fists.

'Yes.' Izzy grinned. 'Take the courage to his doorstep.'

She frowned at both of them, deciding the second bottle of wine was clearly a mistake.

'You need to go to Highgrove, silly!' they both said in unison.

'To the manor?'

'Yes!'

'But…they're going through so much at the moment. To turn up when his father is in hospital and potentially stir things up…'

'To be frank…' Sadie said, sweeping up her glass and necking a gulp '…the way they treated you all those years ago, they don't deserve such thought now.'

Izzy waved Sadie down yet again. 'I get what you're saying, but you have the contact details for their new housekeeper, don't you?'

'Yes, she was friends with Mum and is one of my clients now.'

'Then contact her,' Izzy said. 'Find out the lie of the land and then make a call on it. But it seems to me the only way to prove your love for him and have him return it is to go to Highgrove Manor and declare it, just like he did ten years ago.'

'Only this time it's you outing the pair of you, fighting for you,' Sadie added.

'And what if it's the last thing he wants me to do? What if I'm wrong and he doesn't love me?'

'Is it really going to hurt more than it does now?' Izzy said softly.

Nothing could hurt more, but at least she still had the uncertainty, the teeny-tiny glimmer of hope. If she went there and he rejected her...

'You're no chicken, Jas!' Sadie shot up and plonked herself between them on the sofa, slapping Jasmine's back. 'And it's high time you stood up to those Highgroves and stood up for your heart too.'

'You've really got nothing to lose, honey. Sadie's right on this one.'

'And *I* really need to get a phone and record you saying that,' Sadie said, and Izzy shoved her, their laughter filling the room and fading out just as quickly. Their focus returned to her as they grinned with absolute encouragement.

'You can do this,' they both assured her.

Could she? Did she really have it in her?

But then, wasn't that exactly what she was trying to prove? That their love was worth the bumpy road that lay ahead, regardless of how difficult it might be.

'Thank you, dear.' Freddie's mum gently patted his arm as she took the gin and tonic from him and sipped at it. 'I'm so glad to have you home, it's been very reassuring for me and your father.'

'Where else would I be?'

Ally looked at him over the water she had

opted for in her present condition. 'Yes, where else indeed.'

He gave her a warning look, but her eyes danced in the light of the study fire, her own pleasure at his return very evident, her amusement over his predicament all the more so. He had told her too much, but then his sister had always been adept at reading him and asking the right kind of questions.

'It will be good to have your father home tomorrow,' his mother continued, unaware of the siblings' silent exchange. 'He won't appreciate the changes that need to be made but together we can convince him.'

'Of course.'

'You will stay for a bit longer, won't you, Frederick?'

'Yes, do stay.' It was Ally's way of saying 'I'm not done with you yet,' though he could hardly see what else she hoped to glean. He'd made it clear to her he was a mess and the only solution, the only thing he wanted above all else, was Jasmine. By his side. And he'd made a complete hash of that.

Would she even let him near her again? Would she forgive him for walking away?

'Frederick?'

He looked at his mother's imploring gaze and scoured his brain for the question he was supposed to be answering. Was he staying? 'Yes, of course I will.'

She smiled at him, her back ramrod straight, her posture perfect, even when she wasn't on show and it was just her children with her. He took up his whisky and strode to the fire, leaned his elbow on the mantel as he stared down into the flames. It had been over a week since he'd left her.

Not just left her but left her without any hope. And all because of what? He didn't want to inflict pain on her further down the road. Well, newsflash, they were already in pain, a pain he couldn't imagine getting any worse, and he knew the only thing that would take it away was to have her by his side. To give her—no, to give *them*—a chance.

A chance at the future they'd always wanted. It might be a decade too late but in so many ways they were better prepared for it now. He just wished he'd come to that conclusion before he'd walked away from her and left all that was good in his life back in paradise—*their* paradise.

He threw back his whisky, grimacing over the burn of the alcohol and his mistake.

'What is it, brother?'

He shot Ally another look. She knew well enough what was wrong and she'd already made her thoughts clear. That he was a damn fool. A fool for letting Jas go, a fool for giving up the one true happiness he'd ever known.

'*Alison*, really. It's been a tough week for all of us, I hardly think the question necessary.'

'Sorry, Mother, but we know father is going to be fine. It was a timely warning and one that will see him listening to our advice at last and taking it easy. We've been on him for years and even Dr McGivern was starting to get blue faced.'

'Yes,' she agreed. 'In that sense it will be a blessing. He certainly needs to retire sooner rather than later.'

'It should be easy enough to convince him of that,' Freddie said. 'Now that I'm moving back to Edinburgh permanently.'

Both women choked on their drinks.

'You are?' Ally said, her eyes wide.

'I have a few things I need to tie up Stateside but, yes, I expect to make Edinburgh my home again in the coming months.'

'Well, your father will be most relieved,' his mother rushed out, colour warming her cheeks as her eyes misted over. 'Though he won't appreciate his stroke being the deciding factor.'

'It wasn't. It's been on my mind for a while.'

She narrowed her gaze on him. 'You never said anything.'

'Well, I have now.' He winced at how defensive he sounded but he'd barely slept in a week and it was starting to show. And he missed *her*, really missed her.

'Maybe if you'd said something sooner, this—'

'*Mum.*' Ally's eyes snapped to her, cutting off the blame that was so obviously coming.

'Yes, well,' his mother backtracked, her voice rising a little as she wriggled in her seat. 'It will make a wonderful change, having you home again.'

'It really will,' Ally said, smiling at him now, her eyes full of compassion and understanding and...hope. Did she know his thoughts? That he was this close to fighting for the woman he'd fought and failed to keep before?

The ancient doorbell rang through the house, its sound jarring and unexpected.

His mother frowned. 'Who can that be? It's a bit late for unexpected visitors.'

Grateful for the distraction, he headed to the door. 'I'll go and check.'

'No need, Stevens will get it.'

'I'll go anyway. The last thing you need is visitors at this late hour. I'll send them on their way.'

'Very good, dear.'

CHAPTER FIFTEEN

SHE WAS ABOUT to reach for the bell again when she saw a shadow approach through the small bevelled windowpanes that made up the top half of the heavy wooden door. Her heart fluttered into her throat and she clutched her chest, seeking comfort from the locket hidden beneath the layers of clothing.

Maybe she should have left it until morning. It was getting late in the day and she knew they'd been to the hospital that afternoon, as they had done every afternoon since the Laird had been admitted. She also knew he was doing well or else she wouldn't be here now. But…

She was nervous.

The long approach to the house had given her too much time to think and agonise over her decision, while reacquainting herself with her childhood and her times with Freddie. Scaling the walls that guarded the main house, climbing the trees that lined the winding driveway, sailing on the loch, building a den and enjoying a stolen tin of Maggie's shortbread, and hiding out in the guest house hidden in the hills…

So many happy memories.

But the trees arching over the driveway had never felt more oppressive as she'd driven beneath them. The house in its vast, austere beauty had loomed dark and grey, looking ever more formidable as she'd approached. Even the rolling amethyst hills surrounding it, the pink hue of the setting sun reflecting off the Highgrove loch and the sight of the deer grazing beside it had done nothing to ease her nerves.

Nothing could penetrate the chill in her heart as she'd climbed the broad stone steps, remembering the night she had run down them, unseeing of the ground, the ice as the tears had rolled freely…

But that was then, and this was now. And she wasn't running scared.

She sucked in a breath as the door began to open, raised her chin as her lips parted, ready to explain herself to the member of staff answering, and…gasped.

'Freddie!'

'Jasmine?'

He looked as stunned as she felt. He scrubbed his face, blinked and blinked again. 'It's really you. What are you…?'

He widened his blue eyes at her, their bloodshot state making her want to cry as her hand wavered between them and she fought the urge to reach for him. He'd aged in a week, lines marring his brow, stubble darkening his jaw, dark smudges beneath his eyes and his skin so very pale against the white of his shirt, the black of his suit. Had she got it wrong? Was his father worse?

Finally, she found her voice. 'Freddie, I'm sorry. I had to see how you were, how your father was.'

He looked back over his shoulder into the darkened hallway beyond, stepped forward and pulled the door to leave a narrow gap.

'He's fine, doing much better already. But you...' His words trailed off as he cupped her face, his thumbs trembling as they swept across her cheekbones. 'After all I said, all I did...'

She covered his hands with hers. 'I had to come, Freddie.'

He shook his head, his lips curving into a smile that was all the more powerful for its sorrow. 'I can't believe you're really here.'

'Well, believe it.' She wet her lips, searched his gaze as she admitted, 'Wherever you are is where I belong.'

He closed his eyes, said her name very quietly.

'I'm here to prove to you that we're stronger together, that you don't need to protect us, to protect me. I no longer need you to be our voice. I love you, Freddie, and I want the world to know it.'

She used his decade-old declaration to bring her point home, but as he opened his eyes, all she saw was anguish and pain, his head shake seeming to reject it all. He opened his mouth and she wanted to cover her ears to whatever was about to come, but instead he drew her body against his. Held her tight.

'I missed you, Red.'

She sank into him, her arms wrapping around him as a sob rose up within her. 'I missed you too. I missed you for ten years, I missed you for a week and, still, I couldn't say which one was worse.'

He pressed a long kiss to her hair, his deep breath an audible rasp above her, but no words came. She pulled back, just enough to look up into his eyes.

'Please, give us a second chance, Freddie. We deserve it, don't we?'

He kissed her, his lips soft and urgent at the same time and she allowed herself the pleasure of it, the joy of being in his arms again, of feeling like she had come home, at last.

But she wasn't. This was Highgrove Manor. And he still hadn't verbally given her his love, his agreement, hope…

She dropped back. 'Freddie, pl—'

'Freddie?' The door shifted open. 'Who is—? *Jasmine?*'

Their heads snapped to a gaping Ally in the doorway, her wide eyes the colour of Freddie's, her sleek black ponytail swinging as she looked from one to the other and back again. And then she started to smile.

'Alison! What's going on?' Their mother appeared alongside her, her voice as grand as the pearls and deep blue trouser suit she wore, her greying hair fixed perfectly into the same tight chignon she had always favoured. 'Jasmine? Jasmine *Walker*? What the devil…?'

She half expected Freddie to jump away or straighten, do anything to lessen their embrace, but his arm tightened around her. 'Jasmine and—'

'I can explain,' Jasmine said over him. It was her turn to do the talking. Or at least she thought it was, but where did she start? She'd recited so many versions of this tale in her head and they all evaded her now.

'You'd better come on in,' his mother said, her eyes both hard and confused, before turning away to march down the hall, muttering something about her son's long-awaited return to Edinburgh making much more sense now.

Ally gave her an encouraging smile, her hand reaching out to gently squeeze Jasmine's arm as her other rested over her very pronounced bump. She looked every bit the elegant aristocrat in the navy woollen dress she wore, but her smile had always made Jasmine feel welcome, accepted. 'It's so good to see you, honey.'

And then she was hurrying off in her mother's wake.

Jasmine moved to go after her, but Freddie held her still. 'No, we're not doing this. Mum,' he called after her. 'I'm going to talk to Jasmine in private and we will—'

'*No*, Freddie.' Jasmine pressed her palm to his chest and gave him a hard stare. 'There are things

I need to say and it's important I say them in front of everyone.'

She could do this. She *would* do it. For them.

'You'd best get the girl a drink, Frederick.'

'I love you, Freddie...wherever you are is where I belong...'

His heart beat faster, Jasmine's words repeating over and over in his mind, warming his chest that had been chilled for days. But was she crazy?

After everything that had happened within these four walls, she wanted to come back here and declare it...

The answer was a resounding yes. Everything about her showed determination: striding ahead of him through the hall; entering the room before him; stopping in front of the fire to face the sofa and armchairs either side, one already occupied by his mother.

No hiding, no cowering, only the slightest nip to her lip that told him she was battling nerves. Her freed hair was a mass of colour as the fire danced at her rear, her thick cream jumper swallowing her up, her legs all the more slender in beige leggings and black riding boots. Even with her back straight, her chin raised, she looked petite, but far from vulnerable and never more beautiful to his Red-starved eyes.

He wanted to pull her back into him, whisk

her away, kiss her until nothing else and no one else existed.

'Frederick!' His eyes shot to his mother. 'A drink!'

'I'll sort it,' Ally said smoothly, quick to move. 'Why don't you take a seat, Jasmine?'

Ally offered her a space on the sofa and Jasmine gave her a smile and sat, folding her hands in her lap as she gave him—*him*—a reassuring smile.

'What can I get you?' his sister asked her.

'Whatever you're having is fine.'

'Oh, no, you don't want what I'm having.' She rested her hand over the curve of her belly. 'I'm on the water.'

'Water's fine.'

'Okay.' Though his sister clearly thought something much stronger would be wise. 'Ice, lemon?'

Jasmine smiled at her. 'Just as it comes. Thank you.'

Ally disappeared and Freddie found himself back at the fire, his forearm resting on the mantel, trying to give the impression that all was fine, but he knew his eyes told another story. He looked from his mother to Jasmine, hardly daring to believe that this was happening. That she was here.

But this was Red. *His* Red. She embodied everything he'd loved as a teen and she'd grown into a woman with all the confidence and strength he'd tried to thrust on her before she'd been ready.

And on top of that she was smiling at him, *she* was giving *him* the strength.

The corners of his mouth twitched, the beginnings of a smile he hadn't given in days, and, satisfied, she cleared her throat softly and looked at his mother.

'I hope you don't mind me turning up so unexpectedly…'

He looked at his mother too, the wasp she was chewing putting up a good fight.

'It must be very important.'

'It is, Lady Highgrove, it really is.' She glanced at him and then she sat straighter, angling her body towards his mother.

'First, can I just say I'm so glad to hear that the Laird is recovering well. I was very sorry to learn of his stroke.'

'Thank you. Your concern is appreciated.'

Jasmine gave her a small smile, her eyes sparkling with compassion as she planted her palms on her thighs. She breathed in deep, letting it out slowly. 'I don't want to beat around the bush, Lady Highgrove, so forgive me if I get straight to the point.'

His mother's eyes widened marginally but Freddie's eyes narrowed on his dear sweet firecracker with her blazing red hair and her bright green eyes, cheeks as pink as a rose, lips as sweet as candy. His heart swelled with both love and pride.

She didn't need him to do anything but watch. She didn't *want* him to do anything.

And it was a pretty good job too, because right now he was the one that was weak, utterly immobilised by her. Hanging on her next move, her next word, all her.

'No forgiveness necessary. Please, continue.'

'I am in love with your son,' Jasmine blurted, and his heart leapt with her confession, his smile twitching to life again as she pressed her lips together and bit the inside of them.

His mother gave no reaction at all as Jasmine leaned closer. 'Truth is, I've never stopped loving him. I've loved him for almost all of my life and, frankly, if that's not a good enough reason for me to be worthy of him, then let this be another. I *know* I can make him happy. I will love him, care for him and be there for him. I have no need of your family name, your wealth, your social status—'

He was torn between watching his love declare her feelings for him so passionately and watching his mother's face slowly change. The flickering emotions sweeping across her features were hard to judge, but he knew one thing, she wasn't immune.

'I am my own woman, with my own substantial fortune, and I can stand my ground. I don't need a man to secure my place in this world, but I do need Freddie to make me feel complete. I am lost without him, Lady Highgrove. And if he will have me then I promise to spend my life loving him and doing right by him, in sickness and in health, till death do us part.'

The room fell silent, the pounding of his heart very loud in his ears as he realised that, whatever happened now, nothing would get in the way of them. Nothing.

'Right, what have I missed?' Ally returned, her eyes flitting between all three of them and taking in the weighted silence.

And then he was moving, as fast as his stride would permit. He took Jasmine's hand and pulled her up into his arms.

'If I will have you? Are you crazy?' His words were muffled against her neck as he buried himself there. 'It's me that should be asking that of you after I left you like I did. I'm sorry, so sorry.'

'Stop apologising, Freddie! I want to be with you. I want to marry you. I want to have kids with you. I don't want to waste a second more when we've wasted so many already.'

'I wouldn't say it was wasted, dear.'

They jerked away from one another just enough to eye his mother, who looked as close to tears as she'd been the day he'd returned from the Seychelles.

Ally was still, so still he almost forgot she was there.

'It seems to me you've grown into a fine, independent woman, and you've made something of yourself.'

Everyone frowned, save for his mother whose lips had the hint of a...*smile.*

'It wasn't that we doubted your love for one another all those years ago. You were just too young, too young and too foolish, and too fuelled by hormones. Youngsters just have no patience in this day and age.'

Ally swallowed something that sounded a lot like a surprised laugh.

'I won't pretend that we didn't want more for you, Freddie. It was always the way that we would expect a high society marriage.' She waved a hand through the air like she was discussing something as simple as the weather. 'After all, an arranged marriage never did us any harm and look at your sister too, the picture of health and happiness. But you, you were always one for doing your own thing. From the moment you could walk right up until the day you upped and left for Harvard. Your father and I worried we'd lost you for good.'

He shook his head. 'If you were so worried that you'd lost me, why keep pushing me into a marriage I didn't want?'

'You can hardly expect us to be happy with your bachelor status. Life is hard, Freddie, you need someone to share it with. And you can't blame us for trying to find you a suitable match, it's expected of us to do so. It's the topic of conversation at virtually every function.'

Her eyes lowered to Jasmine, a faraway look creeping into her blue eyes that were so like her son's. 'We never banked on you coming back, though.'

He sensed Jasmine swallow, felt her arms twitch around him as she said, 'There's a bit of a tale to that.'

'Yes, Alison has said as much.'

'She has?' He looked at Ally, who gave an awkward smile.

'I haven't said *that* much, just that M waved her magic wand and brought you back together.'

'And you didn't say anything to me?' he asked his mother.

'I figured you'd say something in your own time, *if* there was something worth telling.'

'I see…' But did he?

'You have to admit, it is kind of like fate,' Ally said wistfully.

'Trust you to believe in fate, little sis,' he murmured, distracted by his thoughts, still trying to gauge his mother's reaction and the battle ahead. If there was to be a battle…

'Your sister makes a very good point. Even you have to admit, dear, that of all the men and all the women M had access to, bringing you both together was nothing short of a miracle.'

Jasmine and Freddie stared at her, their disbelief growing.

'What?' She gave a short laugh, her cheeks colouring beneath her flawless make-up. 'Is it so hard to believe that I can think fate played a hand? I can be quite a romantic…when I want to be.'

Hard to believe? Try impossible.

'Yes, well,' she rallied into the stunned silence. 'Your father is less so. Best to leave him to me.'

And still no one moved.

'Right, Alison, give the girl her drink and let's go and see what Maggie can rustle up for supper. It seems we have a guest for the night. I assume you will stay, Jasmine.'

'I— What?' She dipped in his arms as though her knees had buckled, and he tightened his hold around her.

'That would be lovely,' he said, giving Jasmine the strength that she'd already expended. It was his turn to step up.

'Yes. Thank you, Lady Highgrove.'

'Annie, please.'

Jasmine swallowed. 'Annie.'

His mother paused at the door, turning back to smile at them both, her eyes resting on Jasmine.

'Your mother was always very proud of you, dear, and quite rightly so. Tonight you shine so brightly that your light is sure to have reached her in the heavens.'

The door closed softly behind her and slowly

they turned towards one another. His hands reached into Jasmine's hair as their gazes locked and he witnessed her love for her late mother, for him, for what was to come glistening back at him.

'I love you, Red,' he whispered into that look. 'I've always loved you, and only you. Will you marry me?'

Tears welled in her brilliant green eyes. 'I will Freddie, I will.'

'And I will of course do that again properly, with the ring.'

She clutched his face in her hands, her smile breathtaking. 'I don't need the ring, Freddie, I just need you.'

'Don't let my mother hear you say that because she's going to want me to use Granny's ring this t—'

His words were cut off by her kiss, her passion, her love...

The love of his one and only Red.

EPILOGUE

One year later

NERVOUSLY, JASMINE BIT into her lip as Freddie tugged her away from the doors that led into the manor's great hall. The noise from the other side ebbed and flowed with music and chatter, the clinking of glasses, the sound of laughter. The evening reception was in full swing. Friends, relatives and staff had all gathered to celebrate their wedding.

'Are you sure we should just sneak off?'

Freddie chuckled and pulled her into his chest. 'It's tradition.'

'Making our secret getaway?'

'Yes. And as I have the jet on standby, it would be rude to keep the pilot waiting.'

She shook her head with a laugh, the loose curls framing her face brushing against her cheeks. He looked so handsome, so impressive in full Highland dress, the kilt giving him an edge she could definitely get used to. As for his hair, it was longer, not quite as foppish as it had once been, but the perfect length for her to run her hands through and she did it now. Gazing up at him with all the love she felt inside. 'Since when have you worried about keeping people waiting?'

'Since I was left waiting ten years for you to come to your senses!'

'*Me* come to *my* senses?'

He chuckled deeper, pressed a kiss to her affronted mouth. 'You *and* my parents.'

'Are my ears burning?'

His father emerged from his study, his face as severe as the day he'd caught her stealing Maggie's shortbread and Jasmine smiled at him, her heart softening. Behind that severe look were eyes that now danced like his son's. Yes, grandparenthood had changed him, but even in the last year she'd witnessed him change further. Whether it was the health scare, the change in his lifestyle or seeing his son so happy, she wasn't sure, and ultimately it didn't matter.

She walked up to him and touched a kiss to his cheek. 'I'll leave you to sort out your son. I just need to speak to Annie before we go.'

She moved to leave, and Freddie caught her up, tugging her back. 'Not yet you don't.' He pressed a kiss to her lips. 'Now you may go, but don't be long.'

She laughed. 'I wonder if marriage will teach you patience.'

'Hey, I waited ten years, remember…' he called after her, and she grinned as she pushed open the doors to the hall and scanned the guests.

So many smiles, so much happiness. The room itself glowed in the light of the chandeliers and the candelabras that ran along the panelled walls, illuminating the paintings and tapestries and hunting regalia from yesteryear.

She spied Annie in the corner, chatting animatedly with a glowing Madison Morgan, their talented matchmaker, or fairy godmother as Ally liked to call her...

She joined them with a smile. 'Ladies, Freddie is quite insistent that we sneak away, but I couldn't go without saying goodbye, Annie. Thank you so much for all you've done to make today so very special.'

She pulled her mother-in-law into an embrace, which was readily returned.

'You're very welcome, dear.' She pressed a kiss to her cheek. 'Yet again you have done your mother proud, and Alan and I couldn't be happier. It is us that should be thanking you for giving us Highgroves a second chance.'

The wedge in her throat swelled with every word and as Jasmine leaned back, she saw that Annie too was close to tears. They squeezed one another's arms and she managed a whispered. 'Thank you.'

Then she turned to Madison. 'And thank you too. Without your magic we wouldn't be here now.'

'I'm not so sure...' Madison smiled at her, her warm brown eyes all knowing. 'I think one way or another you were destined to meet again. I just made it happen sooner rather than later.'

Jasmine gave a soft laugh and pulled her into a hug. 'Whatever the case, thank you.'

'You're very welcome. I hope you have a fabulous honeymoon. Has he given away the destination yet?'

'He doesn't need to, there's only one place for us.'

'Ah, of course!' She gave a knowing wink. 'Back to Rosalie.'

'Ooh, you'd better go, dear, your husband is on the prowl and I wouldn't put it past my son to throw you over his shoulder and carry you off.'

She turned to see Freddie stalking towards her, his intent clear in his mischievous grin. She picked up her skirts and dashed towards him.

Yes, she was running, but this time she was taking him with her.

'I'm rea—'

Her words became a squeal as he swung her up into his arms, cradling her body to his. 'I'm done with waiting, wife.'

'Freddie! You can't carry me out!'

'Oh, believe me, I can. I've waited eleven years for this honeymoon, I'm not waiting a second more.'

'But—'

He kissed away her words and she clung to him as the room of people fell away, leaving just her and Freddie and their love that had stood the test of time.

When he eased his lips from hers, she was breathless and flustered and very much in need of the cold outdoors.

'That was rather foolish of me,' he muttered, rapidly striding for the exit.

'Was it? I rather liked it.'

'I rather liked it too…too much.'

She frowned up at him. How could one like a kiss too much?

'Never mind going into battle without undergarments beneath your kilt…' he continued. 'Try kissing your wife a little too deeply in front of an audience…'

She covered her mouth with her hand, tears of laughter and happiness spiking. 'If it makes you feel better, I do love a true Scotsman.'

He clutched her tighter, his grin swiftly returning. 'You'd better.'

'Always, Freddie. Always.'

* * * * *

If you missed the previous story in the Billion-Dollar Matches quartet, then check out

The Princess and the Rebel Billionaire
by Sophie Pembroke

And if you enjoyed this story, check out this other great read from Rachael Stewart

Tempted by the Tycoon's Proposal
Available now!